"*Lucas, it's awfully generous of you to let me stay here.*"

"Think nothing of it. I'm a generous guy."

Sarah smiled. "I know. You're kinda shy, too."

A look of surprise crossed his features. "When you know me better, you'll find I'm not usually at a loss for words."

His modest disclaimer enchanted Sarah. What a sweet man. "You shouldn't feel self-conscious at having softer, gentler qualities than most men, Lucas."

"I—I shouldn't?" He stared at Sarah in absolute stupefaction, astonished by her misconceptions about his basic temperament. Good grief, the woman was looking at him as if he had all the sex appeal of a cocker spaniel—a fixed one, at that.

"Definitely not. Not every man can be Rambo. Besides, the world needs nurturing men."

"Tell me, Sarah. What kind of man do *you* prefer? A Rambo type or... is Mr. Rogers more your style?"

Sarah thought for a moment. "Rambo's always seemed a bit... primal—you know what I mean? I'd much rather have Mr. Rogers over for lunch."

"Then Mr. Rogers it is," he muttered softly.

Dear Reader:

1990 is in full swing, and so is Silhouette Romances' tenth anniversary celebration—the DIAMOND JUBILEE! To symbolize the timelessness of love, as well as the modern gift of the tenth anniversary, we're presenting readers with a DIAMOND JUBILEE Silhouette Romance title each month, penned by one of your favorite Romance authors.

This month, visit the American West with Rita Rainville's *Never on Sundae*, a delightful tale sure to put a smile on your lips. Losing weight is never so romantic as when Wade Mackenzie is around. He has lovely Heather Brandon literally pining away! Then, in April, Peggy Webb has written a special treat for readers—*Harvey's Missing*. Be sure not to miss this heartwarming romp about a man, a woman and a lovable dog named Harvey!

Victoria Glenn, Annette Broadrick, Dixie Browning, Lucy Gordon, Phyllis Halldorson—to name just a few—have written DIAMOND JUBILEE titles especially for you.

And that's not all! This month we have a very special surprise! Ten years ago, Diana Palmer published her very first romance. Now, some of them are available again in a three-book collection entitled Diana Palmer Duets. Each book will have two wonderful stories plus an introduction by the author. Don't miss them!

The DIAMOND JUBILEE Celebration, plus special goodies like Diana Palmer Duets, is Silhouette Books' way of saying thanks to you, our readers. We've been together for ten years now, and with the support you've given to us, you can look forward to many more years of heartwarming, poignant love stories.

I hope you'll enjoy this book and all of the stories to come. Come home to romance—Silhouette Romance—for always!

Sincerely,

Tara Hughes Gavin
Senior Editor

PAT TRACY

Tiger by
the Tail

Silhouette Romance

Published by Silhouette Books New York

America's Publisher of Contemporary Romance

To Sandie Valerie, sister and exuberant confidante

Special Acknowledgment to:

Karen Finnigan and Maxine Metcalf
for their advice and encouragement

SILHOUETTE BOOKS
300 E. 42nd St., New York, N.Y. 10017

ISBN: 0-373-08710-1

First Silhouette Books printing March 1990

Printed in the U.S.A.

Books by Pat Tracy

Silhouette Romance

His Kind of Woman #654
Tiger by the Tail #710

PAT TRACY

lives in Idaho Falls, Idaho, with her three daughters. An essential part of her life is the three-mile country walk she takes each day. During these walks she daydreams of heroes and heroines who dare to commit their hearts and lives to each other. She sees their faces, hears their words, and then hurries home to tell her computer all about it.

She is the winner of the Romance Writers of America's Golden Heart Award for *His Kind of Woman*.

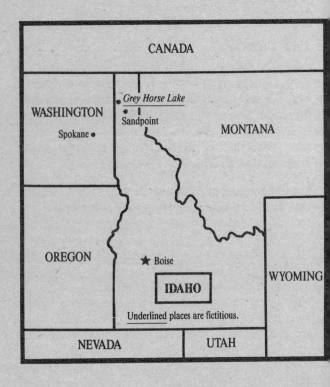

CANADA

WASHINGTON

Grey Horse Lake

Sandpoint

Spokane •

MONTANA

OREGON

★ Boise

IDAHO

Underlined places are fictitious.

WYOMING

NEVADA

UTAH

Chapter One

When she opened her eyes and saw her unfamiliar surroundings, Sarah smiled. Stretching her fingertips, she stroked the taut blue wall of her brand-new tent. The slippery fabric was real. Her smile grew. She'd done it, really done it.

Filled with a sudden burst of energy, Sarah sat up and unzipped her light blue sleeping bag. It, too, was newly purchased, as were her insulated air mattress and the red long johns she wore. Her white wool socks were new, too. She hadn't brought one "old" thing from Spokane. A new beginning—a new life—demanded new things.

At the august age of twenty-six, the only thing Sarah Burke had decided to recycle from her past was...herself.

Humming a cheerful but tuneless snatch of mismatched notes, Sarah scooted to the front of her igloo-shaped tent, unfastened the center flaps and poked her head out. Sunshine smacked her square in the face. Cold sunshine, she acknowledged ruefully, gazing into the early April sky that crowned Grey Horse Lake, Idaho.

She could feel tiny goose bumps rising on her skin. The salesman who'd sold her camping supplies had assured her that, while lightweight, polypropylene was the perfect fabric for camping. Rubbing her palms against her arms, she questioned whether or not the salesman had ever spent a night in the mountains.

She shut the tent's flaps, retreated to her sleeping bag and slipped inside, zipping it closed with trembling fingers. Maybe she should wait for it to warm up before venturing out. She clamped her chattering teeth together and wondered if she'd be waiting until July.

Sarah Burke, are you going to let a little cold keep you in your sleeping bag? It's morning. Up and at 'em.

The distinctive voice Sarah heard from days long past was that of her domineering older brother. Of course, *he'd* never let a cold snap interfere with his agenda. No, Ryan Burke would simply go on about his business—the family business most probably. Burke Realty. Burke Realty—minus the youngest Burke.

As she'd done many times before leaving Spokane, Sarah assured herself that she hadn't really abandoned her family. She was just taking a five-month leave of absence. Anyway, how could a father, mother and brother who were the sharpest, most aggressive real-estate brokers in Washington state possibly need the services of the least effective member of the firm?

Despite her impressive list of sales, Sarah knew she was Burke Realty's weakest link. But that didn't mean she couldn't be successful doing something else. It just meant she needed to strike out on her own and try something different for a while.

Strange how a disastrous love affair could change one's perspective. Sarah wiggled her toes to generate a little warmth. Strictly speaking, her year-long involvement with Ned Ranklin couldn't be called a love affair. They hadn't made love. She had simply admired the sophisticated broker from afar until he'd begun dating, then courting her.

The courtship had been followed by a marriage proposal and formal offer to merge the two competing brokerage firms. She liked to think she would have caught on to Ned's motives before she married him. But she'd never know for sure because her brother had confronted her almost fiancé and steamrolled him into confessing the impending merger of the two firms meant more to Ned than Sarah ever would.

How long would it take her to forgive Ryan for conducting that showdown in her presence?

Suddenly it occurred to Sarah that lying in a sleeping bag and wiggling her toes while philosophizing about life wasn't a particularly profitable way to spend the first morning of the rest of her life.

She pushed aside the sleeping bag again, this time with determination. And when the morning sunshine splashed across her face, Sarah didn't flinch. Instead she savored the beautiful lakeside scenery, future site of Camp Grey Horse.

Then, less than twenty feet away, a black blur of movement snagged Sarah's gaze. Her breath caught in her throat. A small bear cub meandered toward her tent. No heavier than forty pounds, the furry bundle looked like an animated, if somewhat clumsy teddy bear. Instinctively she took a step toward the cub.

"Oh, you adorable baby." Her voice was a soft croon. She didn't want to frighten the button-nosed, chocolate-eyed bear.

Then she stopped abruptly. Baby hadn't been delivered to this clearing via the stork. Baby had to have a mamma. And Mamma probably wouldn't have a cute, black-button nose sitting beneath two friendly, nonthreatening brown eyes. No, nothing about Mamma would be cuddly and appealing. Sarah took two small steps backward, relieved that her presence hadn't seemed to make an impression on Baby.

A spindly pine tree no taller than the cub itself had caught his interest. She let out her breath slowly, retreated another step and then another. Baby seemed utterly content to bat the toddler-size pine within an inch of its life.

When a good thirty feet stood between herself and the cub, Sarah inhaled a deep breath of cool mountain air. Her eyes widened in horror when she coughed. Her citified lungs seemed no match for the rich blend of pine, wild mint and lilacs that permeated the oxygen-thin atmosphere.

Holding her hand over her mouth, she kept her watering eyes pinned on Baby. He was now rubbing his back against the accommodating trunk of a lodgepole pine, still sublimely unaware of her presence.

Dumb cub. Didn't he realize how vulnerable he was? She could understand him not picking up her scent because she was downwind from him. Nor could she fault him for not spotting her vivid red long johns. Bears were notoriously nearsighted. But he should have reacted to the sound of her coughing. And just *where* was Mamma? With her casual mothering technique, she certainly wouldn't be winning any mother-of-the-year awards.

During the past few months, Sarah had done a lot of reading about her new work environment. She'd had to in order to convince Deborah to keep the remote mountain property she'd inherited and go into business with her. The thought of her closest friend brought a pensive frown to Sarah's mouth. Poor Deborah. She had really gone through a devastating series of crises.

The totally unexpected and unnervingly close sound of laughter—human laughter—sent thoughts of Deborah and her recent tragedy flying from Sarah's mind. In the formerly silent clearing, the discordant racket sounded like a cannon blast.

She shot another look at Baby. He had stopped rubbing his back against the rough bark of the trunk and now sat staring directly at her. Standing perfectly still, she held her breath. With the tent between them, most of her bright red long johns were blocked from his gaze.

Nice little bear, don't you pay me no mind. You just go on with what you were doing. Hadn't she read somewhere that thought waves carried energy? As if he, too, had read the same article, the cub directed his attention to the aromatic properties of a nearby wild-flower, dipping his pink snout into its golden interior.

Another tinkling strain of laughter rang out. "Gosh, Lucas, this is great. What a perfect day."

The feminine voice reached Sarah's ears with total clarity, and she had to bite her bottom lip not to call out to the unseen girl that there had been more "perfect" days.

"You're right, I've never seen Gray Horse Lake any prettier. Here, Julie, let me help you from the boat."

The man's deeply pitched voice seemed to fill the open area between Sarah and Baby. Curiously she looked around.

Sarah edged back farther from the now restless cub. Its exploration of the flower forgotten, Baby had begun to pace. A couple more cautious steps in retreat put three more small trees between them. She cast a forlorn glance at her campsite. Her tent, containing her new air mattress and robin-egg blue sleeping bag represented a significant investment to her. She didn't want to desert them.

"It's all right. I've got you."

Sarah's head jerked around. The husky masculine voice sounded as if it were directed at her. Where on earth were the unseen couple? She felt as if she'd stepped into the twilight zone.

"I know I'm safe, Lucas, as long as you're with me."

The voices were coming from beneath her. Sarah took two more steps back, then stood stock-still. There was no more "back" to retreat to. When she looked over her shoulder and down, she was staring at the smooth shoreline of the sparkling lake and at a man and girl walking from a small rowboat beached on the sand.

Sarah was six, maybe seven feet above them, perched on an outcropping of forest tundra. A disapproving growl and the sounds of mountain underbrush being rearranged turned Sarah's attention to Baby. Her eyes widened in horror, and she could feel a burst of one hundred percent pure adrenaline sending her pulse rate into maximum overdrive.

Dear Lord, Mamma had arrived—big, mean Mamma. At least Sarah assumed the giant furry mammal with its pink-bewhiskered snout currently nudging Baby about the clearing was the cub's mother.

Below her the man spoke again. "I know you can't see it, Julie. But the lake is the same shade of blue as your eyes. There isn't a cloud in the sky, and all around us is lush, green forest."

Sarah gritted her teeth. She was about to be devoured by a two-ton rampaging bear, and some stranger oblivious to her plight was giving her a weather report. She felt nervous perspiration bathe her skin. Fortunately the breeze that blew against her was coming from the direction of Mamma and Baby.

She wished she had taken the time earlier to put on her Nike hiking shoes. At least that way, when her mortal remains were recovered, the authorities would be terribly impressed by her practical choice of mountain footwear. But then maybe Mamma would finish off her Nikes, too. The white fangs she was baring looked capable of chewing up a greater section of Spokane.

Again the masculine voice reached Sarah. "Julie, over to our left is a family of squirrels. Can you hear them?"

The girl laughed. "Yes, and smell that pine! Thanks for bringing me out today, Lucas."

"Are you feeling better?"

"Terrific. Dr. Phelps says they'll be able to take off the bandages in a couple of weeks."

The lilt of the young woman's voice drew Sarah's frazzled gaze back to the couple. For the first time, she noticed the narrow white strip of fabric covering her eyes. Dressed in pink slacks and a white sweatshirt, she seemed very young and very vulnerable.

"Those two weeks are going to fly by, Julie."

Despite her predicament, Sarah couldn't help noticing the husky cadence of the man's voice. While she could only see the girl's profile, the man was turned so that his entire face was revealed. It was a rugged, tanned face. Obviously he had spent a lot of time outdoors.

Dark brows framed even darker eyes, eyes that seemed oddly gentle amid such sharply angled features. His nose was generous, slightly bent over its bridge—as if broken maybe more than once. His mouth was narrow lipped and firm, but it seemed to curve tenderly.

Sarah felt her throat tighten. Here she was twenty-six years old, about to be a midmorning snack of two-thirds of a bear family, and all she could think was that she could never remember a man looking at her with that degree of tenderness. Ned Ranklin had certainly never looked at her that way.

The sound of fabric ripping snapped Sarah's thoughts back to Mamma. The mother bear had just put a three-foot rent in her new tent. It took very little imagination to see those same curved claws putting a substantial rent in her. Should she make a run for it? Or should she stay put?

Apparently Mamma still hadn't seen her. The bear batted the blue nylon tent twice more, then lumbered back to Baby. A pine cone currently held the cub's interest.

Sarah moved back another inch on the ledge. Of all the directions she could run, it occurred to her that a six-foot jump downward onto sandy soil might be her best move. She glanced again at the couple. The girl had moved closer to the man.

"Maybe when I get my bandages off, we could go to a movie."

"Sure we can."

"All right! We'll go out for hamburgers first and then the movie. It'll be our first date."

The man chuckled. "We've gone out for hamburgers before."

"I know. With my dad and your sister. I mean a *real* date—just you and me—a man and a woman alone together."

"Wh-what?"

Sarah felt a burst of sympathy for the stranger. Clearly he hadn't realized his young companion was smitten with him. Never had she seen a man so blatantly intimidated by a woman, let alone a girl who looked barely old enough to be a teenager.

"Aww, come on, Lucas. Just because I'm fourteen doesn't mean I don't know what's been happening between us."

"H-happening between *us*?"

"It's love, Lucas. True love." The girl sighed lustily. "It's the birds and the bees, the stars and the moon. It's the fight for love and glory."

"Gl-glory?"

"Oh, don't worry. I know it's too soon to be talking about marriage. I have to graduate from high school first."

"You have to *start* high school, Julie."

"I will, next fall. The way I see it all you have to do is wait for me until I'm eighteen. No sweat."

The man named Lucas looked as if he'd like nothing better than to disappear into a puff of smoke.

Me, too, Sarah thought, her gaze returning to her uninvited company. All she needed was for Papa Bear to make an appearance. Then she'd have the starring role in a sequel to Goldilocks and the Three Bears. Only in this version, the bears would be getting a little of their own back.

Mamma began rubbing against the same narrow trunk Baby had used a short time earlier, and the pine buckled under the additional weight. Sarah couldn't keep from staring at the long, lethal claws protruding from Mamma's oh-so-ample paws.

Her mouth went dry. She told herself that in time Mamma and Baby would go strolling off to their home. All she had to do was stand perfectly still.

"I know waiting will be kind of hard. But no price is too great to pay when you find true love. I won't be dating, either, you know."

The girl's voice had risen in intensity. And Sarah was sure Mamma knew that she and her cub were not alone. The huge mammal had suddenly stilled. Its large, black and definitely suspicious eyes seemed aimed straight at Sarah.

Oh, Lord, along with all her other troubles, was Deborah going to have to cope with her best friend and newly acquired business partner's untimely death?

Sarah tensed, ready to act the moment Mamma moved in her direction. Again she decided her best route of escape was straight down. A six-foot drop to the cove below would take her from the bear's perceived territory. She doubted Mamma would abandon Baby to follow her descent. At least she prayed the mother bear would remain with her cub.

Briefly Sarah thought of her brother. If Ryan could see her now, treed on a narrow ledge—in her red long johns—by a ferocious people-eating bear, he would be absolutely livid. He'd warned her about camping alone at Grey Horse Lake, reiterating forcibly about the foolishness of her arriving before the rickety and ancient cabins could be properly remodeled.

But Sarah hadn't wanted to wait. She'd been eager to set up a command post and survey her and Deborah's new business venture. Besides, a week alone in the wild splendor of the Idaho high country had seemed the perfect antidote for a broken heart.

Sarah muttered a soft oath at her predicament and then immediately retracted it. Mamma bear was returning to the maimed tent.

A hasty prayer sprang to her lips. If she survived this, she would *never* do anything impetuous or impractical again. She'd be the embodiment of prudent, rational behavior. Yes, sir, from now on Sarah Burke would have both feet planted firmly on solid ground.

"Cat got your tongue?"

Lucas stared at Julie's earnest expression and felt his forehead bead with sweat. As a favor to his sister, Summer, he'd been spending a lot of time with her new stepdaughter, Julie. Julie's recent accident coming on the heels of Summer's marriage to Julie's father, Damien, had put a noticeable strain on the newlyweds' first days of marriage.

Damien's exasperating but adorable fourteen-year-old daughter didn't seem the least inclined to share her father with another woman.

But Julie *had* taken a liking to him. And, during the couple of weeks Julie needed to recuperate from the eye damage she'd suffered using a tanning lamp, it had seemed a good idea to invite her to spend some time at his cabin with his housekeeper and his housekeeper's young son.

The idea of including Julie in his vacation plans had seemed a good one. At least better than having Julie accompany Summer and Damien on their honeymoon. But as Lucas stared into Julie's earnest face, he realized his month in the Selkirks wasn't going to be all honey and brightness. He was definitely in trouble—deep trouble.

His new niece-in-law obviously had a crush on him that he hadn't noticed developing. He didn't want to hurt her feelings. Knowing Julie, she'd probably call her father in Hawaii and insist he arrange for her to join him. And that would spoil his sister's honeymoon. On the other hand, he couldn't encourage the girl.

Think man. You're supposed to be such a red-hot administrator. Lucas ran a shaky hand through his hair. He might have a hundred employees scrambling to keep him happy at Rockworth Construction, but that fact didn't seem to cut any ice in his present predicament.

"We could start by going steady."

He cleared his throat but couldn't think of anything to say. Nor could he remember ever feeling as helpless as he did now. All he could do was look into Julie's young face and remember how he'd felt when he'd been sixteen and had a crush on Miss Skagget, the prettiest woman ever to teach math at Lincoln High.

"Ah..." He broke off, having no idea what he meant to say. He looked skyward. What he needed was a bolt of inspiration, or failing that perhaps an earthquake to get him off the hook.

"You do think I'm pretty, don't you?"

Time had run out. He was going to have to handle the situation the way he handled the rest of his life—bluntly. Obviously there wasn't going to be any divine intervention to bail him out.

"What I think is—"

A high-pitched shout cut him off. Lucas glanced up and was stunned to see a woman take a running leap from the ledge above them. He reacted instinctively and held out his arms.

"Lucas, what's going on?"

He didn't let Julie's question distract him. Instead he caught the falling woman, feeling as if he'd plucked a comet from the sky. The spontaneous maneuver wasn't as neatly performed as if they'd rehearsed it, but his reaction time had been quick enough to save the woman he now held in his arms from a nasty spill.

An enraged growl from above made him jerk his gaze upward. An angry black bear stared back at him. And that explained the "why" and "where" of the woman's sudden arrival.

"Don't move," Lucas ordered softly to Julie. "There's a bear on the rise above us."

Julie froze, saying nothing. Lucas's gaze dropped from the bear to the woman he held. He didn't dare let her go. Any movement could prove the catalyst that would bring the bear charging down on them. A sable-colored swath of shoulder-length hair had fallen across the woman's face. Lucas fought the temptation to push back her hair and see what she looked like.

The lady in red ... Somehow the term conjured up images of a slinky, low-cut evening gown instead of old-fashioned red underwear.

"Is Mamma still there?"

Her voice, soft and breathless, warmed him. But her words were chilling. "Your mother is up on that hill with the bear?" he whispered back, without moving his lips.

"Not *my* mother," she corrected quietly. "Baby's mother."

"My Lord, you mean there's a baby up there, too?"

When Sarah had opened her eyes briefly, all she'd seen was her own hair. She knew she was being held in a pair of strong arms against a powerful chest—the chest of the man the girl had called, "Lucas."

She allowed herself a moment of regret that such a strong and virile man, a man endowed with a bone melting deep voice, was also slow-witted.

"A baby bear."

Lucas sighed in relief. "Oh."

Another furious growl ricocheted through the air. All three humans froze while their hearts raced at breakneck speed. Lucas's eyes clashed with the black ones of the bear. His grip tightened on the woman in his arms.

One second ground by. Then another. Finally the black bear's massive head turned, and the rest of its shaggy body followed. In the space above the mountain brush where once death had awaited, there was now only empty space.

The focus of Lucas's gaze returned to the woman. He visually followed the trail of tiny red buttons that led from the V of her legs, past pertly tilted breasts to a crew neck. There was nothing flimsy about her. Hers was the well-toned, faintly muscled body of a runner.

"Is it over? Can I open my eyes?"

He shifted her weight so that he supported her with one arm. With his free hand, he smoothed aside the brown hair that had fallen across the woman's face.

His mouth fell open in disbelief. Never. Never had he believed in fate. And yet cradled protectively in his arms was a woman that for months he'd been unable to get out of his mind.

Carefully he eased her to her feet. The last time he'd seen Sarah Burke he'd told himself it would be a wasted effort to make her acquaintance. The lady was taken.

Chapter Two

Sarah stared curiously into the dark eyes of the stranger who'd saved her from crashing to the sand. Even though he'd let her slide to a vertical position, his arms were still looped around her waist.

He smiled down at her, and his rugged features softened dramatically. She swallowed. All the tenderness she'd wished for moments before spilled from her rescuer's face.

Sarah knew her family had often bemoaned her spontaneous nature, her impetuous habit of jumping to conclusions about people. Had they been present, they would have cautioned that she was in the arms of an unknown man. Measured suspicion would have been their sound advice.

But Sarah's natural inclination was to trust her instincts. And her instincts told her that here was a basically shy man. Hadn't a young girl's crush reduced him to stuttering incoherence?

She smiled warmly. "I think you just saved me from a broken something. Thanks."

"You're welcome."

His voice was deeply pitched, his expression thoughtful. The pressure of his arms gathered at her waist remained firm, and Sarah assumed he was so shaken by their encounter with Mamma that he couldn't move.

The thought of this tall, virile man being over-whelmed by their harrowing experience touched Sarah. Obviously he was a very gentle person.

"You can let go of me," she said kindly, not want-ing to embarrass him.

A look of puzzlement crossed his tanned face. Then he looked down at the hands that spanned her waist. "I suppose I'll have to," he agreed, returning his dark gaze to her face. "For now."

Sarah felt the oddest quiver in the pit of her stom-ach. But before she could ponder the bizarre sensa-tion, the girl with the bandaged eyes spoke up.

"Is the bear gone, Lucas?"

"Looks like it." He slackened his hold on Sarah.

Standing with her arms gathered around herself, Julie looked even more vulnerable than usual. Lu-cas's first instinct was to give her a hug and assure her that everything was all right. But with Julie thinking definitely unniecely thoughts about him, he didn't dare embrace her.

"I—I was so scared. Who are you talking to?"

"Me—Sarah Burke," Sarah answered gently. She'd seen the automatic step her rescuer had taken toward the girl. And she'd seen him stop. She understood his quandary. He had been put in the position of having to second-guess how his every action toward the girl would be interpreted. Sarah's opinion of the careful man went up.

"Where did you come from?"

Sensing the man's discomfort in dealing with the love-struck girl, Sarah took pity on him and decided to rescue him from the awkward situation.

"I jumped down from a ledge above you." She approached the young woman and touched her arm reassuringly. "Your tall friend caught me and probably saved me from breaking my neck. Anyway, Mamma Bear's gone, so you can relax."

Julie hugged her arms more tightly around herself. "I don't think I'm going to be able to relax until we're safely back at your cabin, Lucas. Can we go now?"

"In a few minutes." Lucas took a deep breath before walking over to his new niece. "Here, take my arm. There's the trunk of a fallen tree right behind you. You can sit here while Miss Burke and I make sure it's safe for her to return to her..." His words trailed off, and he considered her form-fitting long johns.

Sarah felt an unfamiliar flush sweep through her. The man's penetrating gaze made her aware for the first time of just how thoroughly the red fabric accentuated her curves.

He continued. "I assume you were camping when...Mamma Bear discovered you?"

His whimsical tone and the sparkle in his dark eyes seemed to increase her feeling of warmth. "That's right, I had just stepped outside my tent when—" She interrupted herself with a wail. "Oh, no! My tent!"

Forgetting everything except the mortal wound Mamma had inflicted on her poor, defenseless tent,

Sarah turned to scale the sloping rise leading to the ledge from which she'd jumped.

"Wait here, Julie. I'm going to make sure Ms. Burke's campsite is safe."

"All right—but hurry, Lucas. This isn't exactly fun, you know."

Lucas swallowed his impatient comeback. He reminded himself that Julie Quincy was only fourteen. She hadn't learned yet that having fun was not a Constitutional right.

"I'll be right back."

His rubber-soled canvas shoes were definitely not designed for climbing grassy inclines, Lucas decided as he followed after Sarah. But then neither were stockinged feet. A mental replay of Sarah practically flying up the face of the small bluff flashed across his mind.

Sarah Burke—leaping small cliffs in a pair of long johns. He couldn't help grinning at the incongruity of that image with that of the last time he'd seen her. The grin died. That was one particular memory he could live without.

He cleared the ledge and stopped in his tracks at the sight that met him. Sarah knelt before a crumpled pile of blue material, looking stunned at the disaster that had befallen her. At his approach she looked up. Shock filled her large brown eyes. Shock and righteous indignation.

Lucas decided Mamma Bear had made a prudent decision in vacating the vicinity. Sarah Burke looked mad enough to throttle the mangy vandal single-handedly.

Her gamine face was flushed with color, and her brown eyes were shooting sparks of golden fire. He assumed her soft lips were mouthing silent oaths. All riled up, Sarah Burke was one hell of a woman.

"I don't believe this! My brand-new tent!" She stood and waved a jagged piece of blue nylon at him. "Do you know how much one of these costs?"

He shook his head.

"Well, let me tell you, it costs a lot." She threw the material down in disgust. "And look what Mamma did to my air mattress!"

A mortally deflated orange air mattress was held up for his inspection. "She . . . she killed it. Oh, no, look at my new sleeping bag!"

This time a much-mauled light blue sleeping bag was dragged out. Sarah held it to her chest as if it were an injured child. "My Slumber Jack. She got my Slumber Jack. Oooh, I don't believe it. All my camping gear, my beautiful new camping gear, has been . . . been pillaged!"

Lucas knew Sarah expected sympathy. And she deserved it. But all he could think about was how appealing she looked as she darted about the clearing, blowing her wispy bangs from her eyes while retrieving her damaged camping gear as if the equipment were family members that had been felled in a Comanche raid.

"She even ravaged my survival handbook," Sarah grumbled, reaching down to pick up a torn page. "I knew she was going to be trouble before I even saw her."

"Mamma?" Lucas inquired politely.

"Yes, Mamma." Sarah stared down at the page she held. "Dumb bear. It's only the first of April. She should have stayed in hibernation for at least another three weeks."

"Is that right?"

Sarah glanced up at him. "Of course. It says so right here on page—" She turned and scooped up a couple of more papers. "On page 43. See, 'In mountain high country, the natural habitat for the black bear, hibernation lasts...'"

Lucas listened to her impromptu reading on the habits of black bears and felt himself charmed. Of all the reactions he might have expected Sarah Burke to feel at the demolishment of her camp, indignation at Mamma Bear's deviation from prescribed bear behavior wasn't one of them.

He remembered the first time he'd seen Sarah. She'd come storming into her brother's office, waving a penalty check made payable to Lucas. She'd been so angry she hadn't even noticed his presence in her brother's office.

"So you see, Lucas... Your name is Lucas, isn't it?" All right, so the man wasn't particularly interested in bears, he could just say so, couldn't he? He didn't have to go into a trance.

"Wh-what?"

"Your name," she prompted, frowning at his blank expression. Mamma must have shaken him up more than she'd realized. She stepped toward him and patted his arm in the same manner she'd patted his young friend. "Say, maybe you ought to sit down for a minute. You look a little flushed."

Dark eyes zeroed in on the slender fingers resting against his green sleeve, then they considered the sympathetic gaze frowning up at him from a concerned face.

"Uh, maybe I should at that. Will you join me?"

A strong hand settled over her fingers, firmly sandwiching them between his warm palm and sleeve. Sarah felt herself maneuvered toward a white granite boulder. The next thing she knew she was sitting beside the shaken man on the smooth rock—her hand securely locked in one of his large ones. Poor guy, it must be tough to look like Rambo and have the soul of Tom Hanks.

She sat quietly, studying the disaster site that had formerly been her camp. She wondered how she was going to survive the entire week before Deborah and her daughter, Wendy, showed up at Grey Horse Lake. Her glance fell on her duffel bag. At least it had been spared. That meant that Mamma and Baby hadn't gotten into any of her dehydrated food packets and wouldn't be returning for additional handouts.

"My name is Lucas Rockworth."

Sarah jumped at the husky murmur inches from her ear, then slanted a look at the man. They were sitting so close she could see the individual spikes of his dark lashes and the tiny lines fanning out from his brown eyes. She noticed the smooth texture of his freshly shaven jaw and the firmness of his narrow lips.

How had he broken his nose? Surely not in a fight. Despite his rugged exterior, Lucas Rockworth didn't appear to have the temperament of a fighter. Of course that would explain the injury to his nose. He hadn't known when to duck. She sneaked a quick glance at his muscular physique. He certainly had all the right equipment. Maybe what he needed was a coach. Someone to—   "Sarah?"

"Hmmm..."

"Where's your car?"

She looked up at him in bemusement. "What car?"

"The car that brought you to the lake. The one that's going to take you out of here now that all your camping supplies have been trashed."

"Would you believe I don't have one?"

He had to smile at her disgruntled tone. "Absolutely. How'd you get here—by parachute?"

"Nothing so dramatic. My business partner dropped me off."

Man or woman? he wanted to ask. "And your partner will be back when?"

"In a week."

Lucas stood. "Well, then, I guess there's only one thing to do."

Sarah stood, too, having no idea what Lucas Rockworth was talking about. She frowned, concentrating on his name. There was something disturbingly familiar about the name, Rockworth. She repeated it in her mind a couple of times. Then her eyes widened. *L. Rockworth!*

He bent over her duffel bag. "Here—catch."

Sarah's hands came up automatically, while her thoughts whirled.

"Nothing else looks worth salvaging. I'll use what's left of your tent to carry out the debris."

She held on to her duffel, watching him methodically pick up what Mamma had reduced to litter. "This is going to sound kinda dumb. But do I know you?"

Lucas paused in the act of rolling up her flattened air mattress. "In a manner of speaking."

Sarah tipped her head, staring at him intently. A feeling of foreboding washed through her. "Could you be more specific?"

"I'm the man you and Burke Realty screwed out of Deborah Scott's lakeside property."

She felt as if she'd jumped off another ledge. The world couldn't be that small a place. "Isn't ... er ... *screwed* a pretty harsh word?"

His eyes glittered. "Yeah, it's a harsh word. But it fits what you did to me after taking my earnest money."

"You got back your earnest money, plus a substantial penalty payment to cover your trouble."

And it was my money! Sarah vividly remembered her brother demanding the loss be covered by her because she'd been the one to talk Deborah out of selling. Ryan had also insisted she pay him the commission he would have earned from the sale, since it was he who'd shown Rockworth the land.

When Ryan had accepted the check to cover his commission, he'd told her it was for her own good. Just as discovering the truth about Ned Ranklin had been for her own good. Sarah had learned to be suspicious of those things in life that were for her own good.

"But I didn't get the property I wanted," he observed ever so softly.

Sarah stood stiffly. "I'm sorry. When Deborah listed that land with Burke Realty, she was in a state of shock because of her husband's death and her daughter's accident. When she regained her perspective, she decided to keep the property."

"So I heard—via her attorney."

"Why are you at the lake, Mr. Rockworth? Have you decided to sue Deborah after all?"

Lucas shook his head, wondering where his sudden anger had come from. He'd already reconciled himself to losing out on the land deal. And he'd bought another site abutting the lake. True, the cabin that came with his new property was hardly the structure he'd envisioned for Deborah Scott's land. But he owned a construction company, and he wouldn't have to compromise too drastically to have a dream version of his second home.

"No, I'm not interested in litigation against Burke Realty." He smiled wryly. "Last time your brother ate me and my lawyers alive. I'm definitely not interested in tangling with him again."

Sarah relaxed. She could identify with how Lucas felt about going one-on-one with Ryan. Her brother was a cold-blooded businessman who didn't believe in compromise. A mild-mannered man such as Lucas Rockworth wouldn't have stood a chance against Ryan.

"Then what are you doing here?"

"Taking a vacation."

"Where?" she asked suspiciously. The other cabins surrounding the lake were all privately owned.

"When your brother showed me the Scott property, I noticed that one of the other summer lodges was for sale. I bought it as a second choice."

"I—I'm sorry for the trouble Deborah's change in plans caused you." The apology came easily to Sarah. The thought of causing anyone pain distressed her.

Lucas had to smile. Despite her contrite expression, he had no doubt that Sarah had a great deal of her brother in her—she was a Burke after all. He couldn't help thinking she'd rip up another earnest money agreement any time it conflicted with what was best for the seller. Tough lady. Tougher than she probably realized.

"Lucas! Lucas, how much longer are you going to be? I'm tired of sitting around waiting for you."

Julie's voice sounded as if she were standing in the clearing with Sarah and Lucas. At its strong decibel level, he did a double take, then flashed Sarah a look of astonishment.

"Before you jumped off the ledge, you heard everything that went on down there, didn't you?" He spoke in a tight whisper.

Sarah nodded, fascinated as she watched a dull flush creep from the collar of his shirt and cover his face. She didn't think she'd ever seen a man blush before. The unique experience confirmed absolutely in Sarah's mind that, despite his rugged appearance, Lucas Rockworth was a shy, sensitive man. A man who might be knowledgeable in the construction trade, but utterly helpless when it came to dealing with women.

"You've got to believe I haven't encouraged her," he explained defensively, picking up the tent into which he'd bundled her destroyed camping gear. "We're coming, Julie. Just hang tight!"

"Oh, I believe you, Lucas," Sarah inserted blandly.

He turned to see if she were being facetious. "You do?"

"Um-hmm. Young girls are notorious for having crushes on older men."

Lucas froze. "How old do you think I am?"

She studied him. "Sneaking up on forty?"

"Thirty-five," he corrected, his dark eyes snapping. "I turned thirty-five last week."

"Happy Birthday," Sarah offered brightly, unable to hold back a grin."

"Why you little—" He broke off. Her teasing rendered him speechless. He'd been running the American division of Rockworth for only a year. Yet he realized in that short space of time, he'd forgotten how it felt to be kidded. He had assumed authority over a hundred people, people who would have cut out their tongues before playfully cutting him down to size.

"Little what?"

"Little vagabond. Come on, let's get Julie back to the cabin."

"You expect me to go with you to your cabin?"

"Got a better idea?"

"Well, maybe not better. But I am going to stick to my original plans. I really don't need a tent, and there's enough left of my sleeping bag to keep me warm."

"The ground's going to be awful hard without an air mattress."

"I'm young. I'll survive."

"This morning's weather forecast said it might rain tonight."

Sarah looked up. "There's not a cloud in the sky."

"And if Mamma comes back?"

She couldn't help smiling at the man's attempt to be assertive. He was a pale imitation of her older brother. "The chances of her showing up again are nil."

"Lucas! Hurry up."

He walked over to the ledge. "I'll be right there, Julie." Then he turned back to face Sarah. "I don't like leaving you here alone."

"I'll be fine."

"But—"

"Go."

Lucas stared at Sarah, read the stubbornness shining in her eyes and shrugged. Come midnight, he had the feeling that Ms. Burke would be singing another tune.

He could have insisted. Her brother would have.

Sarah scrunched deeper into her tattered sleeping bag. First bears, now hurricane-force winds. She clamped her chattering teeth together. Her adventure at Grey Horse Lake was shaping up like a Western saga. All she needed were some renegade Indians to come galloping through her campsite.

The night wind howled mournfully. Noise seemed to leap at her from every direction. And from some demented part of her subconscious sprang fully formed the disturbing memory of the last horror film she'd watched. She'd been thirteen at the time, smart enough to realize the unfortunate family of six wasn't going to stand a chance against an ax murderer.

Don't think about axes and flying body parts. Think about . . . Lucas Rockworth.

She liked him. Despite the heated words they'd exchanged over Deborah's land. Despite the fact he hadn't insisted she return to his cabin with him. What she had liked most about Lucas Rockworth was his sensitivity in dealing with Julie. Clearly he'd been knocked for a loop by the girl's declaration of love. Yet he hadn't come down on her like a ton of bricks.

But if she liked Lucas because of his basic gentleness, she couldn't fault him for not bullying her into going to his cabin with him. Now her brother would have simply picked her up, tossed her over his shoulder and carried her home. Ryan wasn't the kind of man who took "no" for an answer. Regardless of the fact that both their parents were alive and in good health, her brother had pretty much dominated her all her life. Or tried to, she amended.

A furious gust of wind ripped through the clearing, and she drew her knees to her chest, hugging her body heat to her. She tried telling herself that it really wasn't so cold. Besides, she had on her long johns, two flannel shirts, her Levi's, three pairs of socks and her shoes. What more could she want?

Central heating.

This is a learning experience, Sarah. Now you know firsthand how cold it gets at the lake. Look on the bright side. At least it isn't raining.

A blast of thunder rocked the campsite, and Sarah squeaked. There was another cannon blast, and then the rain fell. Gallons of it. Instantly she was drenched.

She stood up, spitting out water. She wanted to swear, to lash out at the nonassertive man who'd left her out here to die. "Oooh, Lucas Rockworth, I—"

"Sarah!"

Strong hands cupped her shoulders and spun her around. "Lucas!" Thank God.

Rain washed down her face and body, collecting in the sodden sleeping bag that had fallen to her knees. She should have been miserable. But she wasn't. Sweet, gentle Lucas had come to rescue her.

"Come on! Follow me. There's a path to my cabin." He had to yell to be heard above the din of the storm.

Sarah pushed her bangs from her eyes. "What about my stuff?"

"I'll take your duffel bag. Leave the rest. It's ruined!" He took her arm, and it seemed she had no choice but to follow.

Chapter Three

When Lucas had used the word *path*, he'd overstated the reality of the all-but-invisible trail. Still, Sarah decided not to hold his exaggeration against him. The hot shower and spare room with its comfortable bed was such a vast improvement over her wet campsite that she could afford to be gracious.

But the following morning her gracious nature did not extend to admiring Lucas's vacation lodge. Once upon a time it might have been considered luxurious. Perhaps when Teddy Roosevelt had presided in the Oval Office, Sarah mused, staring at the knotty pine paneling that seemed to stretch endlessly throughout the cabin.

Surreptitiously she took stock of the run-down interior of a small living room. Actually "run-down" was an overstatement of the room's shabby furnishings and dismal appearance.

If this structure reflected Lucas's tastes, Sarah sympathized with his clients. Hopefully Rockworth Construction merely built houses instead of designing them.

She turned to look out a minuscule window and almost bumped noses with a moose head. Sarah shivered. Poor moose. Not only had he suffered the indignity of being dismembered and stuffed, but he was doomed to gaze forever at his tacky surroundings.

A sagging floral print sofa with holes cut in the armrests to hold drinks, a low coffee table with antlers for legs, and a cuckoo clock with its bird sprung in eternal "koo" constituted the room's highlights.

"It came furnished, Sarah," Lucas observed softly. He'd been standing in the entryway between the living room and the kitchen for several moments, watching the horrified amazement in Sarah's beautiful brown eyes as she surveyed her surroundings.

"Thank heavens." She turned and smiled at him. "I kept imagining your poor customers buying homes like the one the Addams family lived in."

"The Addams family?"

"You remember the television show where they lived in that monstrous mansion with all the cobwebs."

Lucas returned her smile, then looked significantly at the room's bizarre furnishings. "Maybe for one episode they took a vacation and used this cabin for location, hmmm?"

Had she hurt his feelings? Sarah wondered, staring into his dark eyes. After all he had bought the place. "Uh, I wouldn't go so far as to say that."

"I would. This has to be the most god-awful vacation cabin in North America."

"Bu-but you bought it."

"Sure, because I've fallen in love with the Selkirk Mountains and Grey Horse Lake."

"Me, too."

"My architect is arriving in a couple of weeks. Before then, I plan to decide how many walls I'm going to have knocked out and how many terraces the cabin can support. I'm also having a loft added."

"Sounds like an ambitious project."

"I'm an ambitious man."

His eyes caught hers, and Sarah felt a tingly warmth from the waffled soles of her Nikes to her earlobes. Goodness, for a mild man, Mr. Lucas Rockworth packed a real wallop.

She ran her fingertips across her mint green warm-up pants, grateful the housekeeper had run them and her loose-fitting sweatshirt through the dryer.

"I used to be ambitious," Sarah said, wondering why she was suddenly so aware of her body and its working parts. "But I've decided to mend my ways."

"Oh?" One dark brow rose.

"It's for the best," she confided companionably, briefly eyeing the sagging couch and wondering if it would support her hundred-and-ten-pound frame.

Lucas noticed the glance. Sitting with Sarah Burke on a couch suited him just fine. His housekeeper, Tansy, had arrived and was helping Julie change. Tansy's five-year-old son, Ben, was industriously unpacking plastic figures of alien life-forms. Yes, now was a perfect opportunity to get to know the formerly unattainable Sarah.

He reached out and snagged her arm above the elbow, his fingertips sinking into the soft, butter-colored material of her long-sleeved sweatshirt. "Let's sit down and get acquainted."

Sarah felt the pressure of his touch guiding her toward the couch, felt the controlled strength of his muscular body. Since she'd seen how careful and gentle he'd been with his niece, she wasn't the least bit uncomfortable sitting next to a virtual stranger.

"Lucas, it's awfully generous of you to let me stay here."

"Think nothing of it. I'm a generous guy."

Sarah smiled. "I know."

A look of surprise crossed his features. "You do?"

"Um-hmm, you're generous and kinda shy, too."

"What?"

"I couldn't help noticing how embarrassed you were with Julie."

He cleared his throat. "When you know me better, you'll find I'm not usually at a loss for words."

His modest disclaimer enchanted Sarah. What a sweet man. "You shouldn't feel self-conscious at having softer, gentler qualities than most men, Lucas."

"I—I shouldn't?" He stared at Sarah in absolute stupefaction, astonished by her misconceptions about his basic temperament. Good grief, the woman was looking at him as if he had all the sexual appeal of a cocker spaniel—a fixed one, at that.

"Definitely not. Not every man can be a Rambo. Besides, the world needs nurturing men. And you don't have to worry about your problem with your niece, either."

"Why not?" he asked warily.

"Because I'm going to help you off the hook with her. It's the least I can do in return for you giving me a place to stay for the next few days."

"Just one thing, Sarah. What kind of man do *you* prefer? A 'Rambo' type or..." He searched his mind for a quintessential Mr. Nice Guy and remembered the television show his housekeeper's young son liked to watch. "Or is Mr. Rogers more your type?"

Sarah thought for a moment. "Rambo's always seemed a bit...primal—you know what I mean?"

"I'm beginning to get the picture."

"Maybe it's all that sweat..." Her mouth curved. "Or perhaps it's the machine guns. Anyway, I think I'd much rather have Mr. Rogers over for lunch."

Lucas stretched his arm across the back of the couch. "Then Mr. Rogers it is," he muttered softly.

"What?"

"Hmmm? Oh, nothing important. You know you're right about me. I've been battling shyness all my life. Especially around women."

Sarah's eyes filled with compassion. "It's a rough world for a timid man, isn't it?"

"You can't imagine."

Leaning forward, Sarah placed a friendly hand on Lucas's knee. "Your teen years were probably unbearable."

He covered her hand. "I still carry the scars."

A moment of silence slipped by before Sarah spoke. "I suppose we need to discuss tactics."

Lucas had trouble focusing on her words—what with the pressure of her palm on his knee. She was still leaning toward him, her soft lips within striking distance. The scent of her freshly washed hair seemed to enter his body through his pores.

"By tactics, I assume you mean the ones you're going to use to help me discourage Julie."

Sarah nodded, and Lucas congratulated himself on having followed her oblique line of reasoning.

"The thing to do is nip it in the bud before she weaves too many romantic fantasies about you."

"That's bad, huh? Romantic fantasies?"

"Terrible. She'll start seeing you in shining armor, or in a frontiersman's buckskins, or—and this is the worst—a loincloth."

"A—a loincloth?"

"You know, swinging from the trees, all bare chested and free."

Sarah's eyes had taken on a shiny quality that Lucas found fascinating. It was amazing. She had him all hot and bothered, ready to sample the softness of her tender mouth. And yet she seemed totally unaware of him as a man.

"So we want to avoid the loincloth then?" From Sarah's dreamy expression, he'd bet a backhoe that she'd had some pretty sizzling fantasies of her own.

He studied the heightened color staining her wide cheekbones, and wrinkled his brow, trying to picture Mr. Rogers swinging through the jungle in a loincloth. Somehow the image wouldn't gel.

"At all costs," Sarah returned firmly, the trance-like expression fading from her eyes. "But before I can work out our strategy, I need to know what your relationship is with Julie."

Briefly Lucas outlined the details of his sister's recent marriage and her acquisition of a new stepdaughter.

"This could be serious," Sarah observed a few minutes later, digesting what Lucas had said. "Julie's feeling particularly vulnerable. Her father has a new love in his life, and he's left Julie to go on his honeymoon. She's lost her sight...."

"Just temporarily," Lucas reminded her.

"But she's lost her connection with her past, with who she is, and that isn't temporary. You said her father sold the house she grew up in and moved into your sister's condominium. That means a new school for Julie, new teachers, friends—the works. She's suffered a major upheaval in her life."

"I guess I never looked at it that way."

"And then you pop into her world—all tall, dark and handsome. Of course she thinks she's in love with you."

Lucas couldn't help inflating his chest at Sarah's praise. The woman had discernment.

"Of course, she has no idea what you're really like. Her crush has nothing to do with *you*, per se. She sees the macho wrappings and has no idea that inside you're a shy, sensitive man."

"Qualities which you *do* find attractive, right?" He had no intention of hanging on to that sappy image, unless it appealed to Sarah.

As long as he'd been sentenced by his doctor for some short-term R and R in the mountains, he was going to make the most of it. The first time he'd seen Sarah Burke, she'd intrigued him. She was so different from the women he usually found himself attracted to. He was all for broadening his horizons and not averse to a summer romance.

Sarah shifted on the uncomfortable sofa. It was amazing, but sitting next to Lucas Rockworth was beginning to make her heart beat a little faster. Never mind that he had the soul of a poet. He had the rugged body of a warrior. The minute she'd mentioned the word *loincloth*, it had been his tanned physique she'd envisioned in one.

"We're not talking about me. We're discussing Julie."

"I know. But a few minutes ago you said you liked shy, sensitive men."

"No, I said that the world needed more of them."

"Wait a second, Sarah. I distinctly remember you saying—"

She interrupted him, wearing a sad smile. "You misunderstood me, Lucas. The truth is I'm not interested in any kind of man—not anymore."

"What!"

A sheen of watery brightness filled Sarah's brown eyes. "I'm off men."

"Off—off *men*?" His normally deep voice had risen one full octave.

"Uh-mm, I've turned over a new leaf. I'm committing myself to celibacy."

"Celibacy?"

"Goodness you don't have to repeat everything I say," Sarah responded, raising her chin. "Lots of people have decided to take that route. You read about it in the magazines, hear it discussed on the talk shows. It's the new wave."

"Celibacy?"

"It's a viable solution in today's society. That way you don't have to worry about disease or...or..."

"Or?"

"A love affair gone wrong, a...a broken heart."

Immediately Lucas relaxed. So that was it. Lovely Sarah had had her heart broken. She'd been burned. Badly. And she didn't want to get burned again.

"You just need some time. You'll change your mind."

She looked at him skeptically. "I really don't think that's going to happen. Anyway, we seem to have gotten off the subject of Julie's infatuation."

"That we did." He glanced toward the room's small window. "Look, I can feel the walls of this place beginning to close in. "Let's get out of here."

Sarah followed his gaze and encountered the unblinking stare of the morose moose. "I'd enjoy a breath of fresh air."

Lucas's lodge might not have been much to look at, but the site upon which it sat was a spectacular stretch of mountain high country. Everywhere she looked, Sarah saw pines—ponderosa, lodgepole, blue spruce, cedar, Scotch... More kinds than she could put names to.

A nearby meadow had begun to green nicely. All the early tuliplike wildflowers were already in bloom. Yellow, purple and white blossoms poked their bright heads throughout the lush meadow. Darker splashes of green were provided by sprawling bushes that grew in tangled heaps beyond the ankle-deep mountain grass.

"What are you thinking, Sarah?"

"Hmmm?" She turned and looked at Lucas.

"Or should I ask, what are you dreaming, Sarah Burke?"

The mistiness vanished from her gaze. "I wasn't daydreaming. I was thinking, planning actually."

"My mistake."

Sarah began to walk along the lake's sandy shoreline, and Lucas followed. He was surprised when he realized he had to lengthen his stride to keep up with her. Her legs, gorgeous though they were, were definitely no match for his. She was simply in a hurry. He wondered if she knew where she was headed.

Lucas resisted the tiny pang of guilt he felt at misleading Sarah about his basic temperament. But he'd learned in life that man had to take his best shot. Months ago he'd run into Sarah in Spokane, and she'd appealed to him. He'd heard she was engaged and banked his interest. Now fate was obliging him with a month of being close to an obviously *unengaged* Sarah.

Lucas Rockworth had never walked away from opportunity before. And he sure wasn't going to start now.

They'd walked about fifteen minutes before Sarah slowed her brisk pace and then stopped. Still Lucas said nothing. Something was bothering Sarah, eating at her. He could see it in the way her soft lips were pursed, in the way tiny furrows lined her forehead.

She stared out across the restless surface of the lake. "This is where our land starts."

"*Our* land?"

"Deborah's and mine. I hadn't realized it until a few minutes ago, but your property runs right next to ours."

"Is that going to be a problem?" He frowned, trying to fathom the sudden brittle quality of Sarah's voice.

"It might be." Sarah contemplated her other neighbors.

Presently the four luxurious vacation lodges nestled on their two-acre plots were unoccupied. The lodges were immense, multileveled structures with sun decks and towering windows that ran the widths and lengths of the state-of-the-art mountain residences. Sarah knew that shortly their owners, their *aristocratic* owners, would be arriving to enjoy the peaceful splendor of their mountain retreats.

How would they and Lucas react when they learned what she and Deborah had in store for the generous slice of the lake and land they now co-owned?

"I don't see any problem—neighbor."

"Lucas, how do you feel about children?"

She gazed into his startled eyes so she might read the truth of his answer.

"Ch-children?"

"You're doing it again—repeating what I say."

"Sorry. Er, just how many children are we talking about?" *Children? What happened to being celibate?*

"Probably only twenty—the first season."

"Uh, Sarah, are we talking "people" children?" he asked, well remembering "Mamma" and "Baby."

Sarah laughed. "Of course. What other kind of children go to camp?"

"Camp?"

"Lucas..."

"I'm repeating you, I know." He smiled, shaking his head. "Has anyone ever told you that you have a habit of skipping over important details?"

"I know," she acknowledged glumly. "But I'm working on changing."

"Don't work too hard on changing. I like you just the way you are." Good grief, he was beginning to sound like Mr. Rogers.

"You're really sweet, you know?" Sarah stepped closer to Lucas. He wore a dark green, long-sleeved shirt and well-washed jeans. The casual clothes emphasized his muscular fitness. She couldn't help contrasting his well-honed virility against Ned's mildly out-of-shape body.

Then Sarah mentally shook herself. She had no business comparing the physical assets of the men she knew. She was above that sort of thing now. She'd outgrown men, evolved beyond a need for them in her life.

Lucas's smile broadened. "You're an excellent judge of people, Sarah. I *am* sweet, and trustworthy and...I love kids—all kinds, all shapes, all sizes." So he'd only come out at night, when all the little demons were tucked in their beds.

"That's wonderful, Lucas. I was worried the children might disturb you."

"Won't bother me a bit."

Sarah looked at Lucas and blinked. The sun was directly above them now, and its rays seemed to outline his rugged body in a wash of brightness. With the help of Sarah's imagination that brightness took on a silvery glimmer, as if he were garbed in armor, a suit of armor. She blinked again.

"Got something in your eye?" Concern laced his husky voice, and he leaned toward her.

"N-no." His handsome face was so close she could see only the narrowed black pupils of his dark eyes. A gentle mountain breeze caressed them, making her aware of his masculine scent.

"Anyone ever tell you you've got gorgeous, golden, sexy eyes, Sarah Burke?"

She shook her head solemnly. No one had told her, had they? She couldn't remember. Her whole world seemed to have skidded inward to a tiny pocket of the universe that held only herself and this gentle man.

His very closeness compelled her to tip her head back. Her eyelids suddenly seemed weighed down. She could feel them drifting closed.

Her lips tingled with warmth. Slowly they parted— waiting, waiting for... something, anything... everything.

Lucas knew he was being well and truly beckoned. It wasn't wishful thinking that had turned Sarah's gaze to dark honey and opened her full lips in silent invitation.

Sexy little celibate. Sarah's mind might be serious about writing off the male segment of the human race, but neither her heart nor her delightfully formed body was in accord. The setting was right—ripe.... And despite her protests, so was she. Too bad he wanted her mind a willing participant in whatever was going to happen between them. No 'Sorry I lost my head— this must never happen again.' Uh-uh.

He gritted his teeth. So he would retreat a bit, back off and give her some space. He'd already made her aware of him as a man. He could afford to bide his time.

"So you and Deborah Scott have gone into business together, hmmm?"

Sarah opened her eyes and found herself standing alone. Lucas had moved a couple of paces to her right and was staring out across the lake.

She felt the blood rush to her face. Good heavens, what had happened? One moment she'd been a kiss away from ecstasy, and the next she was left to ponder the incredible shyness of one Lucas Rockworth. Sarah was absolutely convinced that it had been his shyness around women that had scuttled the impending kiss. What a dear, sweet man.

And he liked children, too. Maybe if they'd met before her disastrous involvement with Ned, she would have been heart-whole and able to respond to Lucas.

A tiny inner voice inquired what Sarah called her reaction to Lucas—if not response. She hushed the intrusive voice. Lucas needed reassurance. If nothing else, she could use their association to bolster his self-confidence.

She stepped beside him. "That's right. Deborah and I are going to build a children's camp here at the lake."

Awfully expensive property for a summer camp, was Lucas's first thought, but he didn't speak it aloud. He didn't want to say anything that might diminish the excited glow on Sarah's face.

"And you expect to have twenty young campers before summer's end?"

"Yes, isn't that wonderful?"

"Wonderful," Lucas agreed huskily.

"Come on, I'll show you what we've got planned."

She held out her slim hand, and Lucas stared at it for a moment. He was not, had never been a possessive man. And yet when his fingers closed firmly around Sarah's trusting hand, he felt damned possessive. And more than a little uneasy.

She energetically tugged him along a narrow, winding path. Because thick undergrowth and wildflowers covered the low hills rising before them, he reluctantly let go of her hand and followed single file behind her. In several spots along the lake, white sands gave way to the primitive forest. The boundary separating his and Sarah's property was such a place.

"Aren't you afraid Mamma might be lurking about?" he asked, relishing his view of Sarah's charming backside. Darned if she didn't have a pro-

vocative little wiggle—one he suspected she was unaware of.

When his words reached her, Sarah came to an
abrupt halt and he bumped into her. He smothered a
groan. Bumping into Sarah Burke felt better than a
full-fledged "encounter" with another woman.

"Mamma is a black bear and not usually dangerous to people," Sarah began, quoting from memory
what she'd read in her survival handbook. "She only
became hostile toward us because she thought Baby
was being threatened. She didn't get any food, so she's
probably miles from here by now."

"Right. Still, if you don't mind I think I'd feel better if I lead the way." *That way I won't end up tack-
ling you from behind and covering your body with
mine.*

About to argue with Lucas, Sarah changed her
mind. This would be a good opportunity to shore up
Lucas's confidence. "That's a good idea. I'll feel safer
with you in front. After all, Mamma doesn't have a
track record of obeying the rules."

They traded places on the tiny path. "Deborah
Scott's land begins just over that next rise, doesn't it?"

"Um-hmm." Sarah followed Lucas up the hill. All
around them healthy pines stretched skyward.

The faint murmur of the lake and muffled sounds
they made moving along the path fell into a greater
pool of eerie silence. No intrusive noises from the
twentieth century disturbed that pervasive quiet.

To Sarah it seemed as if they could have been a man
and woman from an earlier era, perhaps looking for
a temporary sanctuary. She imagined a scene from a
Western romance. The man would be at home among
his primitive surroundings while his companion would

be unfamiliar with the savage wilderness in which she found herself. She'd stay close to her man.

And he would move with sure-footed courage, fearing no wild beast nor Indian. He'd be carrying a long-barreled rifle with which he was a deadly accurate shot. He'd have an ugly-bladed knife, too—strapped inside his leggings. He'd be wearing buckskins, of course. They'd have been given to him by the fearsome tribe of bloodthirsty Indians who had raised him from boyhood and called him Lone Brave With Doe Eyes That Flame.

"Is that it—the site of your future camp?"

Before Sarah let go of her daydream, she took a second to appreciate the breadth of Lucas's wide back. His well-fitted shirt gave her a clear view of the powerful muscles that had enabled him to catch her when she'd come crashing down on him. She sighed softly.

Then she joined him on the hill's crest. "Isn't it beautiful?"

Lucas followed her stare—across the silver beach, over a lush meadow—to a dozen sagging, long-ago abandoned motel units. If they'd been horses, they would have been put out of their misery and shot. Not one thing had changed since Ryan Burke had first shown him the very exclusive mountain property with the crumbling bungalows.

"Beautiful doesn't begin to cover it," he observed dryly.

"I know. Sometimes there just aren't enough words, are there?"

Lucas shook his head, imagining a bulldozer clearing away the useless rubble. Following the dozer he'd have two work crews going twenty hours a day to erect his beaut of a summer lodge. "No words at all," he agreed.

Sarah moved past him, running down the overgrown path that led to the meadow. Lucas doubted the soles of her canvas hiking shoes touched earth.

"Are you coming?" Sarah stopped and stood with her hands on her hips.

"Definitely."

"Well, hurry. I want to show you the most darling little motel in the world."

"How far a drive is it?"

She laughed at him. "There's no drive, silly. You're already looking at it."

Silly. He smiled crookedly. No one had called him that since he'd been four. "Sarah Burke, even you can't call those pitiful log bones, 'beautiful.'"

"Oh, but they are! We're going to remodel each and every one of them from the inside out. We're going to keep all the gingerbread trim and paint it white. Each of the little cabins will be a different color. Deborah and I figure we can put four bunks in each unit. We'll build a big central lodge with a kitchen and common eating area, and we'll have a huge rock fireplace too. We're going to keep horses, so we'll need a stable."

She turned to face him. "It's going to be wonderful. Just you wait and see."

Damned if he couldn't see it—just as she described it. Standing beside her, he caught a glimmering fragment of her dream, and more. He visualized Sarah surrounded by a flock of giggling children. She'd be sharing her own special brand of magic with them.

"It'll be everything you say." He ran a few quick computations through his mind, adding up the costs her dream would incur before it was realized. He wondered if she understood just how steep a price tag she and her friend were going to run up.

She turned to him, suddenly serious. "Lucas, do you realize how unique you are? Most men, my brother, father and Ned Ranklin included, would be trying to figure the cost of this project. They'd be claiming this is prime recreational real estate, far too valuable to build a summer camp on. And here you are in the construction business, and you haven't said one word about building costs."

Lucas ran a forefinger around his open collar. "Uh, well . . . There *is* a place for practicality—"

"But not for you—right? The most important thing to you is people's feelings."

"Well . . ."

"Oh, don't feel you have to spout some macho diatribe. I've got your number, Lucas Rockworth. You're a bit of a softie and a dreamer, too."

"No one's ever actually come out and called me that, Sarah."

She continued, not hearing his disclaimer. "Before I decided to change, lots of people called me a dreamer."

"Change?"

"Um-hmm. My dreaming days are over, Lucas. Deborah and I are going to have a solid business here. Oh, we know we won't begin to break even our first year. But we have enough money set aside to cover all the remodeling and operating costs for a couple of years. By then we'll definitely be in the black. We'll be a bona fide commercial enterprise."

"Bona fide, huh?"

"You bet. And we're giving our camp a different twist that will attract a wide clientele."

"And what's that?" *Spiked cocoa?*

"It's going to be a camp that accepts disabled children. We're going to have wheelchair ramps, therapists and a program geared for both fully active children and those with physical limitations."

"I see." *Commercialism at its fiercest, all right.*

"It will give disabled children the opportunity to mingle freely with children they're often segregated from. We'll be overcoming a lot of prejudices and opening up the worlds of all children."

"I'm sure you'll fill every one of your vacancies."

"Thank you, Lucas. Your opinion means a lot to me."

Lucas had assumed the buzzing hum he heard had something to do with Sarah's softened gaze. He was wrong.

"Oh, my goodness, look at the size of that bee!"

"Oh, Lord."

She looked up at Lucas's pale expression as he watched a furry bee the size of a mature hummingbird buzz them. "Just stand still. It'll fly away."

"I certainly hope so. My epinephrine injector is back at the cabin." He hated admitting this new weakness to Sarah. She seemed bound and determined to peg him as a . . . a sissy.

"You're allergic to bees?"

"Oh, yeah—and I didn't bother to poke my epi-pen in my shirt pocket. The snow's barely melted; I wasn't expecting bees."

His answer came through tight lips, and Sarah assumed he was paralyzed with terror. Good, if he continued to stand still, the bee would leave him alone.

Unfortunately the bee had other ideas. Persistently the furry insect tried to go through Lucas instead of around him. Sarah swallowed. She wasn't allergic to bees but the one presently doing a drum roll on Lucas's shirt front had a stinger on him ample enough to handle a major blood transfusion. She raised her hand and gently tried to nudge it from Lucas's chest.

"What are you doing?" he demanded uneasily, his voice low.

"Trying to get him past you and on his way home. Turn sideways—maybe he'll go around."

Lucas turned. The ferocious bee buzzed louder, angrier. "He didn't like that, Sarah."

Again the huge bee batted its head against his green shirt.

"I think he's trying to pollinate you, Lucas."

"Well, great." He couldn't keep the sarcasm out of his voice.

"Shh, he's getting mad. You're not cooperating."

"How am I supposed to do that?"

"I don't know. Oh-oh, Lucas, I think he's backing up to make a dive. Let's get out of here."

She grabbed his hand and together they ran across the open glen. Hearing the crazed bee in hot pursuit, he and Sarah zigged and they zagged. At some point he realized he no longer heard the homicidal bee. It didn't matter. He'd never felt as good as he felt running through a glen with Sarah Burke.

They were in the middle of the meadow when Sarah felt herself stumble over a path of uneven rocks the new grass had concealed. The rich green ground came up fast. Lucas's body seemed to embrace hers, and both of them rolled over and over across the lush field.

When they stopped rolling, Sarah was anchored firmly beneath him. Lucas's handsome head blocked out the noon sun. His eyes shone hot. And Sarah learned a 'gentle' man could hunger. She felt a sweet contraction in the feminine heart of her.

Her hands crept to his shoulders and then around his neck. She learned something else. It didn't matter. It didn't matter that she'd sworn off men. Lucas's narrow-lipped, sensuous mouth was lowering toward her. *That* mattered.

Perhaps she'd been a bit hasty in renouncing male companionship. Other men might be hard, driven by greed and dominating. But this was Lucas. It was Lucas who brushed his mouth against hers—once, twice, thrice. Then he covered her lips with his. And all her thoughts, confusion and plans quite simply disintegrated.

Lucas felt Sarah's sweet, urgent response beneath him. His last coherent thought, before he surrendered to her feminine ardor, was that being a "nice" guy carried some tasty rewards.

Chapter Four

Magic.... The rush of passion Lucas stirred inside her felt like magic. His solid weight and tenderly aggressive lips seemed to pull her deeper under his spell. And the heat of him, the scent and taste of him contained a binding power greater than any spoken incantation.

When his mouth moved from her throbbing lips, she felt his heated kisses at her cheek, forehead and throat. His murmured praises sent a quiver racing through her. Then all at once, the intensity of Lucas's passion began to overwhelm her. How had this happened? How had this gentle, shy man so quickly overcome his natural reticence?

"Lucas?"

He answered with a steaming kiss, his hands sweeping with fierce determination across her, moving inexorably closer to her breasts.

"Lucas!"

"Sarah, you feel so good. I want to—" He broke off and let his hungry kiss tell her what he wanted. His hands tightened at her rib cage.

She told herself she would enjoy one more kiss before ending this astonishing interlude. She owed it to herself to understand what she was giving up. Somehow being celibate and denying herself kisses and embraces from the likes of Ned Ranklin was an altogether different proposition than denying herself Lucas's delicious caresses.

Then all conscious thought splintered into nonexistence when Lucas shifted their positions. Suddenly it was he who lay against the grass with her sprawled across him.

"Oh!"

"Oh, yes, honey." His fingers tangled in her hair, and he exerted the necessary pressure to bring her mouth back to his.

Too much. There was too much passion, too much hunger, too much intimacy for Sarah to accept. She stiffened above Lucas and pulled her mouth free. The magic had disappeared.

Breathing raggedly, she stared down into intense eyes that spoke both elegantly and primitively of male desire. She watched in fascination as Lucas deliberately banked his smoldering hunger and marveled at how quickly he had sensed her retreat. His hands fell to his sides, and his faintly swollen lips formed a straight line.

When she realized it was the eager assault of her own lips that had caused the sensual fullness around his mouth, Sarah flushed. "Wh-what happened?"

An earthquake. Lucas gazed up into Sarah's astonished face and felt like laughing. And shouting.

And...crying? What was he doing? He'd let his fantasies about an unknown woman hurl him into a never-never land of physical desire. And the first time he found himself alone with the fantasy woman, he'd practically raped her.

No, not rape. She had been wholly willing and cooperative. It had only been when he'd dropped all restraint that she'd pulled back from him. He narrowed his gaze, assessing the brown eyes filled with shock, the passion-bruised lips still parted in wonder and the olive-toned cheeks bathed in a coral blush.

She wasn't ready for him. His mouth tightened. He wasn't ready for her. Lucas tried to tell himself that it was her obvious inexperience that had made him draw back instead of pushing his advantage. But honesty compelled him to admit he felt more than a little overwhelmed by the feelings Miss Sarah Burke invoked within him.

In all the times he'd thought of her, he'd thought of his strong physical attraction. He'd thought of how best to develop an intimate relationship with her. Not that he considered himself a womanizer. But his past involvements with women had consisted of several months of commitment, a mutually enjoyed affair and then a gradual lessening of involvement.

He'd never broken any woman's heart, nor had he had his broken. He had assumed, when fate had so obligingly delivered Sarah into his outstretched arms, that his relationship with her would follow that same predictable course.

Only something had gone significantly wrong. His feelings for Sarah seemed more intense than those he'd felt for any other woman.

He was thirty-five, old enough to make a permanent commitment to a woman. And there was no doubt Sarah had him smelling orange blossoms and trying to remember if his tux was in his closet or at the cleaners.

He wasn't ready.

He'd already accepted he had one demon too many to conquer. The truth was he'd never be ready for a woman like Sarah.

But she was still spread deliciously across him.

"I think what happened was that we, er, *I* got a little carried away." He smiled apologetically, waiting for Sarah to move.

"Oh." Disappointment filled Sarah's voice. She wondered why Lucas's terse explanation seemed so deflating.

She became aware of a strange lethargy claiming her muscles, and she knew it was time she removed herself from Lucas's supine body. Instead she rested her arms across his broad chest and cradled her chin on her hands, meeting him nose to nose.

She wanted to find the words to let Lucas know that, despite what had happened, she still wanted to be his friend. Being such a sensitive man, her drawing back from his kiss could damage his ego. He was probably putting on a brave front to cover up his embarrassment. "You're a very good kisser, Lucas."

"Thank you." And because he couldn't help himself, he began to stroke her back, enjoying the soft texture of her yellow sweatshirt and the firm flesh beneath. "You're pretty good, too.

She smiled. "I—I rather surprised myself. I guess that's what made me pull away from you—my own insecurities. I wouldn't want you to think it was anything you did."

Lucas bit back a groan. He might have intellectually decided that he needed some breathing space between his libido and Sarah, but his body was going quietly crazy at having her draped across him. And to have Sarah sweetly praising his kissing skills was a delicious torment he didn't think he could long endure.

"I appreciate your vote of confidence." He forced himself to stop caressing her. "Uh, I suppose we should be getting back to the cabin. It must be time for breakfast."

Sarah blinked at Lucas's abrupt tone. She interpreted his briskness to be a defense mechanism. He was camouflaging his embarrassment at her rejection.

Short of initiating another round of kissing, she didn't know how to reassure Lucas of his attractiveness. Since she feared where another foray would lead them, Sarah settled for merely patting Lucas's shoulder.

"You're right. I just realized how hungry I—ow!"

"Sarah, what's wrong? Did I hurt you?"

Burning pain stabbed at Sarah's bottom. She jumped to her feet. "Ouch! Oh, that hurts!"

"Sarah, tell me what's wrong." Lucas's voice vibrated with command.

Through watering eyes, Sarah met Lucas's sharply etched features.

"He got me, Lucas. That crazy bee stung me."

"Let me see." He pushed aside her hands.

Sarah responded automatically to Lucas's rough command. It was only when she noticed the strong male fingers pulling down the elasticized waist of her green warm-up pants that she balked.

"Hey, wait a minute, I—" Her protest froze in her throat. Lucas's determined hands had already exposed a shocking portion of her lavender bikini panties.

"Now's no time for modesty," he growled, peeling down her silk undies to reveal an expanse of bare hip marked with a swelling purplish bruise. "Damn, he really did a number on you. The best thing we can do is get some mud on it to draw out the venom."

Lucas jerked out a clump of grass by its roots and a sizable chunk of dark earth came with it. He sprinted to the sandy bank and dipped the grass into the lake. Seconds later he was beside her, pressing the wet, muddy roots against her burning skin.

Sarah might have protested again, but with the application of Lucas's makeshift poultice, the burning magically subsided. It seemed foolish to be embarrassed when Lucas's quick thinking felt so good. She rested her forehead against the mildly scratchy fabric of his shirtfront.

"How you doing? Still hurting?"

Sarah rubbed her cheek against his chest, enjoying the scent of Lucas's woodsy after-shave mingling with his perspiration. "No, the mud seems to be working."

"Let's give it a few more minutes to draw out as much of the poison as possible."

The antiseptic salve Lucas's housekeeper, Tansy, came up with when they returned to the cabin didn't deaden the pain from the bee sting as effectively as the mud had. But the salve did allow Sarah the freedom to enter the kitchen without a hunk of dirt attached to her hip.

Lucas and his new niece, Julie, sat at an immense round table while Tansy shuttled back and forth from a nearby counter. The fiery-haired housekeeper and Lucas looked up when Sarah stepped into the room.

Lucas pushed back his chair and stood. "Feeling better?" His dark eyes studied her thoroughly.

Sarah flicked a quick glance to Julie and noticed the young girl's frown at Lucas's gentle question. "The mud and Tansy's ointment seemed to have done the trick. I pronounce myself cured."

Lucas pulled a chair from the table for her. "Have some of Tansy's flapjacks, and you'll be ready for anything."

Sarah accepted the chair, sitting gingerly toward one side. Lucas's hands settled for a moment on her shoulders and he gave them a gentle squeeze. She sucked in her breath at the delicious tingle his touch unleashed, doubting she'd ever be ready for this gentle seductive man.

Lucas reclaimed his chair. Immediately Tansy set a plate of fluffy flapjacks in front of Sarah. She buttered the steaming stack and helped herself to the pitcher of hot syrup. The delicious pancakes dissolved in her mouth.

Tansy could cook. When she'd first seen the young and shapely housekeeper with green eyes, flawless complexion and cap of auburn curls, Sarah had wondered if perhaps the woman's looks were what had gotten her the job with Lucas.

Sarah had realized at the time her doubts were petty and unfair. And before she'd met Lucas, she would have never entertained such unworthy suspicions. Interesting how a noble man could inspire ignoble thoughts.

"Lucas is right, Tansy—these are fantastic."

The housekeeper smiled warmly. "Thanks. There's plenty, so eat up."

Sarah did just that. As she ate she noticed that, unlike the rest of the cabin, the kitchen had been remodeled more than once during the past century.

Looking around the airy room equipped with a four-burner gas range, indoor barbecue center, microwave and huge refrigerator, Sarah relized why Lucas hadn't simply torn down the existing cabin to build a new one. This room alone was worth thousands of dollars.

The lodge's previous owners had made a major investment in the kitchen—in the form of oak paneling, glass-shelved windows, yards of wood-grained counter space, new stone flooring and an immense oak table. She wondered if those owners had sold the cabin because they'd gone bankrupt remodeling this one room.

While she ate her breakfast, Sarah listened to Julie cajole her uncle.

"Lucas, take me swimming today—*please.*"

Sarah met Lucas's dark gaze over Julie's blond head. Both realized if he took the sightless girl swimming, she would require his undivided attention.

"I'd planned on sketching some preliminary drawings for my architect."

"What am I supposed to do while you're doing that?"

"I thought you might enjoy lying out on the sun deck and putting on your headphones."

Julie's down-turned mouth informed everyone what she thought of that idea.

"You said you wanted to work on your tan," Lucas reminded her.

"I could do that in Hawaii with Dad and Summer, Lucas. I thought you brought me to your cabin so we could spend time getting to know each other."

The girl's threat was implicit. *Humor me, "Uncle" Lucas, or I'm going to crash Dad's honeymoon.* Sarah flashed Lucas a sympathetic glance. He did have his hands full with the lovesick girl. Cautiously Sarah decided to enter the discussion that was in fact a contest of opposing wills.

"I realize you don't know me, Julie. But I'd like to go swimming this afternoon. We could go together—after the lake has a chance to warm up."

The girl bent her blond head and nibbled her lower lip. Her answer came in a low voice. "I don't need a baby-sitter. If Lucas can't tear himself away from his sketches, I'd just as soon be in Hawaii."

Lucas tried to suppress the wave of impatience he felt at Julie's youthful selfishness. One collect telephone call to Damien would bring him to his daughter's side. Lucas had to find some means of placating the girl without leading her on, ripping out the telephone or tying her up. In short he needed a miracle.

"Julie's right, Lucas."

His head snapped up at Sarah's words. He couldn't believe she would side with Julie's childish pique. "Is she?"

"Absolutely. It'd be much more fun if all of us went swimming. Why don't you spend tomorrow working on your designs? Julie and I can pitch in and help

Tansy with the dishes. That way we can all head for the lake." She glanced across the kitchen to where the housekeeper stood at the sink. "Does your little boy know how to swim?"

Lucas watched Tansy nod. His housekeeper's eyes sparkled with amusement as she, too, apparently comprehended how neatly Sarah had rearranged what would have been an intimate interlude between himself and Julie.

"Ben's only five, but he's had swimming lessons." Dipping her hands into the sudsy water, Tansy laughed. "He hasn't quite mastered how to swim more than four feet in any direction, but he's got splashing and floating down to a science."

"I know how to swim but I've never had to do it as a blind person. You'll stay close to me, won't you, Lucas?"

While Lucas searched his mind for an innocuous reply, Sarah answered. "We'll all stick close to you, Julie."

"Gee, thanks."

Instead of acknowledging Julie's facetious response, Sarah directed a question to the housekeeper. "When's a good time for you to go to the lake, Tansy?"

Lucas settled back in his chair, letting Sarah and Tansy set in motion the plans for the day. He reached for his glass of orange juice. Evidently Sarah had been serious when she'd offered to pay for her week's stay with him by discouraging Julie's crush.

So Sarah Burke kept her word. Interesting.... He thought back to how she'd jumped into the conversation to bail him out when Julie pressed too hard. It occurred to him that each time Sarah had come to his defense it was because she thought he couldn't handle an amorous fourteen-year-old girl.

Sarah thought he was shy. Sensitive....

The night at Grey Horse Lake was everything Lucas had hoped for when he'd made his second-choice purchase of the cabin. He liked the silence and the solitude.

Not wanting to disturb Tansy or Ben, he kept his tread light as he descended the back steps of the cabin. He'd turned over the two bedrooms on the lower level of the cabin to them. Since their rooms were the closest to the back door, he made a point of moving quietly.

He wasn't surprised by his inability to fall asleep. Since his return to the States, he'd had an ongoing battle with insomnia. No wonder Sarah had thought he was almost forty. No.... He wasn't ready to think about Sarah. That was for later. Later when he'd walked off some of the nervous energy he could feel coiling inside him.

He ran a hand through his hair and kept walking. The moon was a bright spotlight against a backdrop of silver-studded blackness. He had no difficulty finding and following the path to the lake. If only he could find with equal ease the path to end the competitive rivalry his father felt toward him.

He had thought he'd found a way to blunt that rivalry when he'd gone overseas. But Lawrence Rockworth had been the original force that had built Rockworth Construction on two continents. And Lawrence Rockworth made a point of measuring his son's successes against what he himself had accomplished at the same age.

And so, even with an ocean separating them, Lucas had had to tolerate his father's almost pathological competitiveness. The solution had been there, of course. Lucas had been aware of the solution since he'd been twelve and his father had virtually sold him as slave labor to a construction job that had required him to work ten hours a day, alongside seasoned carpenters. Every summer after that Lucas had worked other construction jobs.

And always the solution had been there. Three words to his father would have ended the bone-tiring labor. But the three words would have choked him. *I give up....*

Lucas bent down and picked up a handful of small rocks. He threw one, then another and another into the lake. *I give up....* He hadn't been able to say the words when he was twelve, but he'd been ready to say them to his father when he was twenty.

I give up, you can have the damn business, the glory—the money, all of it. I'm leaving. There's a big world out there and I can do any damn thing I please in it—and be a success, a bigger success than you ever thought of becoming.

He'd been ready to say the words, ready to grab the solution and never look back. But there had been Summer. He wouldn't abandon her to their father's biting temperament. It had been when he'd imagined taking Summer and himself from his father's sphere of influence that Lucas had discovered the single truth he supposed he'd known for years but never acknowledged.

It would break his father's heart if he lost his son and daughter. Lawrence Rockworth was a ruthless, selfish bastard the world had knocked around, until the day he'd come out swinging to build his construction empire. But underneath the harshness, underneath the inarguable ambition and grit, was an aging man who'd lost the ability to maintain a single friendship. Aside from his two children, he was utterly alone. He had his millions, he had his power, he had his . . . empire. And he was alone—but for Summer and Lucas.

Lucas had discovered he could no more abandon his father than he could have abandoned Summer. So he'd gone to Europe to put some physical distance between them, let Summer carve out a niche for herself in the computer end of the operation and hoped to hell there was some way for him to end up a different man than his father. "Like father, like son," people often said. But to Lucas, it was a curse he wouldn't voluntarily accept.

He scooped up another handful of rocks. So who were his friends? He could count them on one hand— the good ones, the ones who could meet him as equals and not expect any handouts. Was he on his way to becoming like his father? He let the rocks fly and subsequent splashes followed in rapid-fire succession. He had the ambition. He could feel it in his blood, in his marrow, in his soul. He wanted more. He wanted bigger. He wanted better.

He stopped himself from grabbing more rocks. That was what Grey Horse Lake was all about—his experiment with premeditated relaxation. His doctor didn't like his blood-pressure reading, didn't like his cholesterol levels, didn't like the interior condition of his stomach. Hell, probably the only thing about him that brought a smile to Dr. Eric Royden's patrician features was the promptness and size of the checks he received from Rockworth's insurance carrier.

Slow down, Lucas.... Slow down and smell the roses, Lucas. You're a dead man if you don't slow down....

Lucas grabbed more rocks, holding them tightly in his fist. Well, he'd surrounded himself with a whole damned mountain of flowers and grass and trees and for good measure—a lake. And earlier today he'd run across a meadow, hand in hand with a dark-haired angel.

Just thinking about Sarah eased the tension from his body. Choices and solutions. He could go on the way he'd been and meet up with a genuine, card-carrying angel. Or he could make a few concessions and have his dark-haired one.

If he had the courage to take her on her terms.

He wondered if Sarah realized the kind of terms a woman like her could demand from a man. He felt the corners of his mouth curve into a rueful smile. Probably not. She wouldn't be tossing around the word *celibate* if she did.

The smile faltered, then died. Ned Ranklin had put that word into her vocabulary. Lucas thought back to the last time he'd seen Sarah Burke, before plucking her from the sky.

He'd walked into the crowded, noisy gala Quincy Enterprises was hosting for area builders, bankers and Realtors and looked straight past Summer on Damien's arm. Across the room had stood Sarah Burke. Bone-jarring lust had caught him by the throat—not to mention a few other vital organs—and refused to let him go. He'd had to remind himself to keep breathing.

At first he hadn't recognized the dazzling woman standing some twenty feet away from him as Sarah. His stare had been taken up with feminine curves covered in shimmering silver. The dress she wore had been designed with one purpose in mind—to drive men wild. Simple sequin straps, a plunging V neck and the figure-hugging caress of spun silver...

Then he'd realized the woman was Sarah. His eyes had recognized her anyway; it had taken a moment for his brain to catch up. The simply cut swath of sable hair, the wide cheekbones, provocative mouth and large brown eyes had emphatically informed him he was looking at Sarah. He remembered snapping his mouth shut while fighting the asinine urge to cross the room and throw his dinner jacket across her bare shoulders.

He'd taken three steps toward her, then stopped when a look of adoration had swept her features. For one crazy instant he'd thought the look was for him. Then his brain had kicked into gear for the second time that night, and he's seen that Sarah was leaning back into the dark-suited support of an obliging male.

He'd watched Sarah tilt her head toward the formerly unnoticed man. Lucas was close enough to hear Sarah's soft laughter. Close enough to see her lips place a kiss on the man's jaw. Close enough to realize she was in love.

He'd recognized her companion as Ned Ranklin, as greedy and ambitious a businessman as had ever squeezed a fortune from the lucrative Spokane area. It had taken ten full beats of his heart to exert the control necessary to turn away from the couple.

He lived in modern, civilized times. He had no hidden fortress in which to barricade a seized woman. So the woman who attracted him was in love with another man? Why should that disturb him? After all, he was interested only in the short-term.

And the long-term? He stared across the moon-streaked lake. He didn't believe in it. He was too much like his father....

Deny it.

He couldn't. His father had never loved anyone more than his ambition. Lucas remembered the stoic woman he'd called Mother until his tenth birthday. He'd thought his mother was almost as strong as his father. He'd been wrong. Beatrice Rockworth hadn't lived to see her thirtieth birthday.

Lucas felt the night breeze against his face. He hadn't thought about his mother in years, hadn't admitted how much like his father he feared he was becoming.

He'd let Sarah Burke believe he was an altogether different man than he was. Mr. Rogers... He scowled.

Sarah was not a woman who deserved to be trifled with. And he was a man who only trusted himself to... trifle.

An idealistic, warm woman like Sarah needed the caring man she mistakenly assumed him to be. A man for the long haul.

The amazing thing was that when he was around her, she made him feel as if he could be that sensitive kind of man.

Wrong, Lucas. You're turning out to be the kind of ambitious tyrant your father is.

So he'd lost his judgment for a couple of days. No lasting damage had been done. He'd let Sarah spend the rest of the week at his cabin. And while she waited for her business partner's arrival, he'd encourage her to occupy herself by chaperoning him and Julie. From the looks of things, she'd do a competent job.

Absently Lucas brushed his palms against his jeans. The distant hoot of an owl barely pierced his thoughts. He would stop fantasizing about Sarah. Stop picturing her in his bed wearing nothing but a satisfied smile. Stop dreaming about the taste and texture of her skin. He would forbid himself the right to touch or kiss her. For this one week of his life, he would be strong, noble.

Lucas turned toward the cabin. He'd only taken a couple of steps up the path when a shadowed movement several yards away stopped him. Perfectly outlined in silver moonlight, a woman walked slowly toward the lake.

She looked naked.

Elemental.

Sarah.

She paused at the lake's liquid edge for a moment, then moved slowly into the dark water. The moonlight haloed her in silver.

Sarah silhouetted in silver.

How could he resist?

Lucas moved purposefully toward her, smiling grimly. In five seconds, he'd discovered with irrevocable certainty that he hadn't a noble bone in his body, that he was probably a bigger bastard than his father, and there was no way he could walk away from a silver-drenched, wet and naked Sarah.

Chapter Five

The lake was cool, not icy. Sarah stepped into its silver-frosted waters and savored the coolness. Her bee sting had begun to throb.

Earlier she'd applied a wet washrag against the sting, and it had lessened the throbbing—temporarily. She'd tried pacing her room, but it was darned hard to pace on her tiptoes. Julie's bedroom was on one side of her, and Lucas's room on the other. She hadn't wanted to disturb either of them.

But when she'd slipped into bed, sleep had eluded her. Then she'd moved to a window and gazed out at the lake. Its mountain waters were tempting, and Sarah hadn't thought twice about yielding. She'd pulled her pale pink maillot and pair of sandals from her duffel bag and purloined a fleecy bath towel. Minutes later she'd crept through the cabin and followed the path to the lake.

The full moon had made everything easy. If she'd had to hunt up a flashlight, she probably wouldn't have seized the moment and sampled the lake's midnight allure.

The water felt wonderful—cool, wet and soothing. She waded out until the lake hit her waist high and then sank to her knees, letting the water rise to her shoulders. Using the balls of her feet she pushed off and floated on her back, gliding silently toward the lake's center.

She supposed it might be dangerous swimming alone at night, but she wasn't concerned. She knew herself to be an excellent swimmer. She'd never had a cramp in her life, and no people-threatening critters frequented mountain lakes. She felt safe, protected by the quiet shore and nearby pines. Besides, anything that felt this wonderful couldn't be bad.

Sarah's thoughts drifted like the water that embraced her. The evening's solitude was quite a change from this afternoon's visit to the lake. A telephone call to Julie's doctor had kept the girl out of the water. The physican had warned Lucas that Julie would be risking infection if she got her bandages wet. Julie had not accepted her disappointment well. Even though Lucas had spent a hefty chunk of time with her, she'd worn a petulant frown most of the day. Lucas hadn't seemed all that cheerful, either.

Cool water flowed over Sarah's shoulders, down the valley between her breasts and across her stomach and legs. Slowly it nibbled into Sarah's consciousness that much of what she thought she knew of Lucas was only through her own intuition. She smiled. Her intuition might have failed her with Ned Ranklin, but she was certain she was right on target with her impressions of Lucas Rockworth.

Sensitive, sweet and wonderful... That summed up Lucas very nicely. Lazily she moved her arms and continued propelling herself across the deepening water. The throbbing in her hip had disappeared.

Several months ago when she'd decided to embrace celibacy, she had thought she'd hit upon a marvelous solution for avoiding heartbreak. Tonight she wasn't so certain. What would it be like to have a gentle, caring man in her life? Not someone like Ned or her brother, Ryan, who tended to dominate people and manipulate the circumstances around him. But someone with a sensitive soul and wellspring of tenderness. Someone like... Lucas?

How long would he be vacationing at the lake? She'd like his advice on having the cabins remodeled. Then there was the design and building of a main lodge and stables. The man owned a construction company and had a scheduled appointment with an architect. Soon he'd have a work crew at the lake. It stood to reason that with advance planning Rockworth Construction could help build Camp Grey Horse.

And she'd be spending a lot of time with Lucas....

"Mmmmm," a dreamy sigh floated from her lips and was swallowed by the night. Slowly she turned, angling her direction back to the shore.

"Having fun?"

At the unexpected sound of Lucas's voice, Sarah stiffened and promptly sank. She came up seconds later treading water with a vengeance and sputtering. "*Where* did you come from?"

"Shore obviously."

In the brilliant moonlight, Sarah could clearly see Lucas's sharp features outlined with beaded water. She shivered. Somehow the night made him seem more stranger than friend.

"Obviously." She dipped her head underwater and then reemerged with her hair slicked back from her face. "I still would like to know how you swam up to me without making a single sound."

"I didn't want to spoil your reverie. I swam most of the way underwater."

"Sneaking up on someone when they think they're alone is a good way to give that someone heart failure." Sarah's heartbeat still hadn't returned to normal. Lucas's sudden appearance from nowhere had jolted her.

"You deserved to be shaken up after pulling a stunt like swimming by yourself at night. What if you'd had a cramp?"

Lucas's tone was mild, but Sarah heard the displeasure simmering beneath.

"I'm a competition-class swimmer, Lucas. Want me to show you?" She had only been dog-paddling to save Lucas the ignominy of her outswimming him. But his relentless harping on a subject he had the nerve to be right about was galling.

Lucas's manner might be unassuming, but his words carried those same overprotective sentiments she'd come to resent. It was her opinion that the "nice" man needed taking down a peg or two.

Lucas laughed. "Yeah, Sarah. Show me your stuff."

She proceeded to do just that. Full tilt. Arms and legs working in smooth, rapid tandem. Facedown, knees locked, palms cupped. The rhythm burned. She took great pleasure in the stoking of it. Faster. Smoother. Stroke after stroke. Clean. Crisp. Faster...

When her feet touched the sandy lake bottom, she was actually disappointed. She'd just gotten warmed up. She waded proudly the rest of the way to shore, bravely ignoring the cooling breeze that nipped at her wet, exposed flesh. Shivering would diminish her victory.

"Very good, Sarah. I'm impressed. You probably could have swam back and forth across the lake all night without tiring. Still it wasn't smart of you to be out alone."

Sarah stopped and pivoted on the sand. When she turned she was surprised to see Lucas standing right behind her. Two thoughts registered simultaneously: Lucas Rockworth was a superb swimmer, and he was naked.

She jerked around, bringing both palms to her flaming cheeks. At least the coolness of the night had stopped bothering her. There was heat aplenty zinging through her racing bloodstream. If she wasn't careful she was going to get a sunburn—from the inside out.

"I apologize for my state of undress, Sarah. Mind if I use your towel? I didn't think to bring one with me."

Apologize for what? For having a gorgeous chest, rigidly flat stomach, firmly muscled thighs and...and the rest of what had required some careful chiseling on Michelangelo's part to finish his *David*.

"You see I thought you were skinny-dipping. It seemed dumb to get my underwear wet when I knew—" He broke off for a moment, then continued. "I'm sure you get my drift. You can turn around now, Sarah. I'm decent."

When she followed his suggestion, Sarah couldn't keep from lowering her gaze. She caught the small "oh" in her throat before it could escape. Lucas was as decent as he could be in a snug pair of white cotton briefs.

Lucas felt Sarah's timid but avid gaze on him. He had no recourse but to turn his back to her—quickly—and reach for his pants. He tossed the slightly dampened towel to her over his shoulder.

"You better dry off. It's chilly out tonight." *Chilly like hell. You're on fire, man. Maybe you ought to swim a couple of more laps.*

Lucas couldn't decide if he was more aroused by having Sarah look at him or by him looking at her feminine curves outlined in her high-cut French-designed maillot. At least he knew now what she did to keep in shape. She was a swimmer—a damned good swimmer. Competition class, she'd said, and she hadn't been bragging.

Sarah rubbed the large towel over her, then wrapped it around herself. A small smile teased her mouth. Lucas didn't fool her for a minute. He'd just been acting casual about his naked and near-naked states. But when he'd turned his back to her, Sarah realized the old, shy Lucas was back.

"You're a pretty good swimmer yourself, Lucas." She brushed a few clinging particles of sand from her feet, then slipped on her sandals.

"Thanks. I've always considered swimming a viable life sport." Lucas didn't add that he swam mostly between two and three in the morning when he couldn't sleep. He bent down to retrieve his shirt from where he'd tossed it.

Sarah sighed, watching Lucas pull his shirt over powerful shoulders. He definitely needed a little excitement in his life—something to enliven his prosaic ways of looking at things. Swimming, a viable life sport, indeed! He made it sound as appealing as cod-liver oil.

"Is that why you bought a cabin on the lake? Because you like to swim?"

"And fish and hike. And then there's all the peace and quiet mountain areas are renowned for."

Sarah wrinkled her nose. "You sound like you're describing a medical prescription."

Lucas startled her by reaching out and running the pad of a callused fingertip across the curve of her shoulder. "Do I?"

She shivered at his touch and turned toward the cabin. As she walked, she could feel tiny flecks of sand rubbing against her feet. The friction of the sand chafing beneath her sandal straps and the spiraling tremors caused by Lucas's touch formed a strange counterpoint of sensations.

Suddenly Sarah found herself wondering about Lucas and women. Despite his shyness, a man as good-looking and virile as Lucas could probably have any woman he wanted.

Most places Sarah frequented in Spokane seemed inhabited by hordes of sexy, chesty women. Would any of those ladies have enough depth to see past Lucas's handsome exterior, to the sensitive, caring man beneath?

No! They'd just enjoy themselves and him on a superficial level. Then the wantons would go on to some other man, some other adventure, casting poor Lucas aside.

She glanced at him as he fell into step beside her. Had he ever had his heart broken? A slow-burning anger rose inside her. Just the thought of Lucas being hurt by a shallow...sexpot stirred within her a fierce cord of possessiveness. She hadn't realized that her fingers had curled into fists until Lucas reached out to take her hand.

"I guess for me the peace and quiet is a kind of medical prescription. My doctor told me to slow down, to—" Lucas broke off with a hollow chuckle.

"To what?"

"To smell the damned flowers. Lord, you'd think with the money I'm paying him, he could come up with something more original than what you'd read on a dollar greeting card."

Sarah stopped and turned to face Lucas. "Are you sick?" She directed a concerned gaze across the length and breadth of him. "You don't look sick." She stepped closer. "Is it your heart?"

Lucas smiled, shaking his head. He couldn't believe he'd mentioned his health to Sarah. He'd told no one about the results of his last physical. He wondered if it showed a weakness of character on his part to enjoy knowing Sarah was concerned about him. "Just a touch of hypertension—"

Sarah interrupted. "That's serious, isn't it?"

"It's the kind of thing that could be serious, if it were neglected. I have no intention of neglecting it."

"Lucas, this is terrible."

"Hey, I'm all right."

"Well, of course you are—now. But what happens when Camp Grey Horse is overflowing with laughing, shrieking children? Where's all your peace and quiet going to be then?''

He shook his head, and she answered for him. "Gone, kaput, splitinsky."

"Splitinsky?"

"You got it." She stared at him in concern. "I wonder if headphones would work."

"Headphones?"

"Headphones—and stop that."

"What?"

"Repeating me. Listen, we could record the forest."

"Record the—"

"Ssh, don't interrupt. That's it, we'll record the forest onto cassettes. You can wear headphones and listen to whatever it is we managed to record. That way Grey Horse's campers won't spoil your peace and quiet. Well, what do you think?"

"How do the words, 'it's so crazy, it just might work,' grab you?"

"I don't know, Lucas. That sounds like something I might read on a dollar greeting card. Can't you be more original?"

Lord, he couldn't remember the last time he'd felt so good. Where had his dark mood gone? "Lots of deep philosophy on some of those cards."

Sarah laughed. "You bet there is."

They fell into step together, walking toward the cabin again. "Are you planning on returning to Burke Realty in the fall?" For some time, Lucas had wanted to know the answer to that question.

"I'm not sure. I'm getting pretty tired of being outclassed."

"I can't imagine you ever being outclassed."

"Sure you can. Just visualize my parents and Ryan. At the first of every month, we start out with a clean slate. And at the end of the month, I'm always in the fourth position. It's so darn frustrating! Mom, Dad or Ryan each take turns being number one, or two, or three. But you can always count on good old Sarah to bring in the rear."

"Does your family stress the competitive factor?"

An edge had crept into Lucas's voice, but Sarah didn't notice. She was too caught up in the injustice of her situation.

"They don't have to. I've got eyes. I can read the monthly reports. It's obvious they've been carrying me. I just don't fit in."

"So you're giving up?"

Sarah didn't like the way Lucas worded his question. It made her sound like a quitter. "I'm opening my eyes and facing reality."

"You set a pretty demanding yardstick to measure your successes by. Your father and mother and Ryan all have reputations for aggressive salesmanship. Being number four in your family is no disgrace."

"In my family, number four is last. I'm tired of being last."

The cabin was in sight. She quickened her step, feeling uneasy that she'd shared so much of herself with Lucas. She was convinced her family thought of her as a vivacious bubble head. She'd never felt close enough to them to share her doubts and fears. They all seemed so strong, so invincible. If she confided her insecurities to them, they'd lose what little respect they did have for her.

Lucas's hand caught Sarah's arm before she could climb the back steps. "I think you're being too hard on yourself. If you were as inadequate as you think, your family would have never let you into the business. Burke Realty has a solid reputation. From what I saw when I dealt with Ryan, he'd never risk that reputation by letting an incompetent into the family business.''

Sarah tried to absorb what Lucas was saying. With the pressure of his strong hand against her bare arm that wasn't easy. She struggled to resist the urge to lean into him, to rest her head against his broad shoulder. The deep timbre of his voice seemed to stroke her body with the gentleness of a lover's caress. She was tempted to prolong this moment with him, to not only hear his caress, but to also feel it.

There was a lump in her throat, and she could feel the liquid heat of unshed tears fill her eyes. What was wrong with her? She wanted to throw herself into Lucas's arms and hear more of his husky words of encouragement. She wanted to feel his mouth on hers again. She wanted to be held—held until the first rays of the morning sun filtered through the pines.

She shook her head, trying to clear her whirling thoughts. But she could find nothing to focus on, save the solid pressure of Lucas's hand. She stared up at him, in mute confusion, scarcely comprehending the myriad of conflicting emotions churning inside her.

Why did she look into Lucas's face and see dark shadows, demons of hunger *and*...solace? It didn't make any sense. None of her thoughts did. She shook her head again. ''Wh—what?''

''Just one kiss, I promise. To hold us till morning.''

Lucas pulled her the short distance into his arms. He hadn't buttoned his shirt and Sarah found herself pressed intimately against his naked chest. Her hands came up. To resist? It didn't seem so. She could feel the muscular strength of his shoulders beneath her fingertips.

His lips were first cool then...hot. Hot like the sun on her bare flesh when she'd laid out for hours. Hot like the lick of a flame at the tip of a match. Hot like—

It was over, the summer storm spent. Lucas drew back, and Sarah dropped her hands from his shoulders.

"Good night, Sarah." His voice was low, gritty.

"Aren't—aren't you coming in?"

"Later."

"Oh. Well, then . . . Good night."

She turned and ascended the back steps.

Lucas watched the door shut behind her. *Damn fool thing to do. Swim alone at night.*

He walked slowly, thoughtfully along the path. What did a man who had never believed himself capable of love do when he found a woman who tempted him to risk everything—his heart, his sanity, his soul—on a gamble for love?

Lucas shrugged off his shirt, then unsnapped his trousers. The lake was calm and as still as a painting. Smoothly he shucked himself naked.

Damn fool thing to do.

But necessary.

"Watch me! Watch me, Mommy!" Ben's exuberant voice rang out with childish glee.

Already dripping wet from his last belly-flopping descent into the lake, the carrot-topped five-year-old made a running leap off the weathered boat dock. His child-size life jacket kept him afloat.

Standing several feet away in waist-deep water, Sarah turned to Tansy. "You're right. He's got floating and splashing down to a science."

The housekeeper's green eyes sparkled with motherly affection. "That's my boy!"

"Did ya see me, Mommy? Did ya?"

"You bet I did, honey. You were great!"

Sarah watched Tansy swim the short distance to her son and became aware of a peculiar ache of emptiness. What did it feel like to be a mother, to be fully responsible for the creation, birth and care of a miniature human being?

Sarah cast a fleeting glance at Lucas. He and Julie were sprawled on beach towels that had been spread across the white beach.

Sarah began to wade toward shore. It was time to liberate her host. As she walked across the more shallow water, she became aware of Lucas's dark stare.

She didn't understand why she found it impossible to meet that stare. Nor did she understand why she felt so sensitive to his gaze. She was wearing the same swimsuit that he'd seen her in last night and yesterday. Her suit wasn't particularly daring. And yet she couldn't shake the impression that when Lucas looked at her, he was seeing her without even the meager covering of pink spandex.

And then there was the matter of her looking at him. She couldn't seem to affix her gaze on anything above his shoulders or below his waist. Oh, she knew he was wearing black swimming trunks. A quick peek had netted her that discovery. Except perhaps, "trunks," was an overstatement. What Lucas wore was black, synthetic and...brief. Very brief. In fact she wouldn't be a bit surprised if his swim trunks were more revealing than his cotton underwear had been. She tried to remember....

Sarah, you've no business trying to remember what Lucas Rockworth looks like in his underwear.

"Hi, Sarah. Lake warming up?"

Lucas's lazily drawled question brought a flush to her cheeks. At the moment she wasn't sure if it was the lake or herself that was the more thoroughly "warmed."

"It's still a little on the cool side, but really refreshing. Why don't you find out for yourself?"

"In case you haven't noticed, Sarah. Lucas is keeping me company."

Sarah took a moment to survey Julie before replying. The girl wore a modest one-piece suit with a ruffled skirt.

"I've noticed, Julie," Sarah said, making an effort to keep her tone neutral. "But I thought I'd talk Lucas into joining Ben and Tansy while I stretched out on his beach towel and warmed up."

Lucas uncoiled to his feet. "Sounds like a fair trade. I'm ready to show Ben my super-duper, rotating triple-axle...belly flop."

Sarah laughed softly and couldn't resist looking into Lucas's smiling face. She felt the laughter fade. His mouth was curved in an innocent smile, but his eyes spoke of needs not quite innocent. She swallowed. She'd spent a large part of this afternoon wishing she and Lucas could play together in the lake's blue waters.

With startling suddenness it became clear to her what form that "play" could take. His strong body brushing intimately against her, his hands...touching her, his eyes…holding her. She looked away from his imprisoning gaze and edged past him.

Fortunately the strength in her knees lasted until she reached his towel. Then she sat down abruptly. "Sounds like you're going to make Ben's day."

Lucas grumbled something under his breath she couldn't quite catch, and then he waded out into the lake. Sarah stared after him. How did he do that? Reduce her to quivering nerve endings with just a simple look? It was a good thing that Lucas was such a thoroughly nice man. Decent. A less-principled man might try to take advantage of her attraction to him.

Sarah reached for the amber bottle of suntan oil that lay a few inches away. Maybe she shouldn't have told him she was celibate. Maybe—

"Well?" Julie's voice snapped Sarah's attention back to her companion.

"Well, what?" Sarah asked, suppressing a smile. Julie Quincy was wearing a rather fierce expression. Sarah sensed that her time on Lucas's beach towel wasn't going to be particularly restful.

"When are you going to start trying to be my friend?"

Sarah yawned, then stretched her arms skyward. "How about in an hour?" She uncapped the bottle of oil, and the scent of coconut joined that of pine and lake. She began to spread the oil on her legs. "I'm kinda sleepy. I think I'll take a nap."

Julie continued to sit stiffly next to her. "You don't fool me a bit."

Sarah laid back against the towel and squinted toward the lake. Lucas, Ben and Tansy were embroiled in a fierce game of water tag. Apparently Lucas was "it," and he only had eyes for a squealing, giggling Ben.

When Sarah didn't reply, Julie continued. "You want Lucas for yourself, so you're going to try to turn him against me. And all the time you're trying to get him to fall for you, you're going to pretend to be my *friend*."

"Am I?" Sarah asked gently.

"That's what women always did when they were after Dad." Anger and bitterness filled Julie's young voice. "That's what Summer did. And now she and Dad have gone off together and left me alone."

Shading her eyes, Sarah studied the angry, disillusioned girl. She felt a burst of tenderness toward the teenager. Julie was only fourteen, and the grown-ups in her life expected her to behave in a rational, adult manner. She was supposed to accept without question her father's right to fall in love and remarry. She was also supposed to adjust to a new mother, new house and new school.

Sarah shook her head, wondering how a bunch of supposed adults could be so indifferent to the cataclysmic changes being forced upon Julie.

"No one ever said life was fair, Julie. It looks like both you and I want the same man. We can be civilized about it and get along with each other while we each set out to win him, or we can follow Plan B."

Young Julie's mouth fell open. "Wh-what's Plan B?"

Sarah dropped her voice to a sinister whisper. "That's where I get you alone and threaten you with blackmail so I can have a clear path with Lucas."

Julie gasped.

Sarah bit back a chuckle and closed her eyes. The sun's rays felt wonderful against her skin—rather like Lucas's kisses of last night.

Suddenly a delighted giggle escaped Julie. "For a minute you had me going. There's absolutely *nothing* you could use to blackmail me."

"That squeaky clean are you?"

Julie nodded, still smiling.

"There's always Plan C."

"Which is?"

"I sneak into your room while you're asleep and pour honey over you."

"And," Julie prompted when Sarah didn't elaborate.

"Well, it's ugly but effective."

"What?"

"Army ants—a whole battalion of them."

"There aren't any army ants in Idaho," Julie protested.

"There're bears."

"You expect a bear to walk up the cabin steps, turn a doorknob and then go up a flight of stairs, find *my* room and attack me?"

"Could happen."

"Only in a movie."

"Hmm, I guess you're right. We just better stick to my original idea."

"I don't remember what that was," Julie confessed, still smiling.

"You and I keep up surface appearances and act friendly while each of us tries to razzle-dazzle your uncle."

"He's not my uncle," Julie corrected quickly. "Not really. His sister just married my dad. That's not the same as being blood relatives."

"Too bad. It'd be easier for me if there was some law prohibiting you two from getting involved."

"Do you... Do you love him awfully much?" The smile had disappeared from Julie's soft mouth.

Sarah sat up. She'd been playing a game with the girl, trying to disarm her with humor. Sarah's eyes focused on Lucas as he roughhoused with Ben. Somehow the serious cast of Julie's question chased away the lightheartedness of the moment.

The logical, rational answer was no, of course she didn't love Lucas. She hardly knew him, had just met him a couple of days ago. She couldn't love him. Even a reformed dreamer such as herself couldn't fall in love that quickly.

"Well? Do you?" Julie persisted.

"I'm not sure," Sarah replied, too shaken to be less than honest with her companion.

Julie's face took on a mulish expression. "Thank you for being honest. I appreciate you talking to me woman-to-woman. And I agree with your suggestion."

"What suggestion?" Sarah asked absently, unable to tear her eyes away from Lucas's strong body. He played with Ben so carefully, splashing up great mountains of spray but directing them away from the laughing boy's face. A gentle man.

"To be mature about this situation. I have the advantage, you know."

The feminine purr in Julie's voice riveted Sarah's attention back to the young woman. "What advantage is that?"

"I *know* I love Lucas."

"And?"

"And as each of us takes turns trying to seduce him, I guarantee *I* will come out the winner of your challenge."

"Wait a minute. I wasn't challenging you."

"Sounded like it to me. And to show you how confident I am, you can spend the rest of the afternoon with him."

"I can?"

Looking fully relaxed, Julie laid down on her beach towel. "But don't you dare come into his room tonight."

"Why not?" Oh, dear, she didn't think she was going to like Julie's answer one bit.

"Because tonight is *my* turn."

Sarah's stomach took a depressing plunge. She didn't think Lucas was going to like Julie's answer any better than Sarah did. And when he discovered it had been something she'd said that Julie had twisted into a...a "tournament of seduction...." he might be just the teeniest bit upset with Sarah.

Chapter Six

You've already done a lot of preliminary work on Camp Grey Horse. It looks good."

"Thank you." Sarah smoothed a creased corner of one of the drawings spread across the kitchen table. "Before we can get started on the construction, we have to wait for the snow to melt. Deborah and I've used the time to work together on the drawings."

Leaning over the sketches, Lucas stood close to her chair. He pointed to the stables. "Both of you have a knack for design. This is the perfect place for the stables. You've got them set back from the lake, on a stretch of level ground, within easy access to the hills that border your property."

When Lucas leaned across the table, Sarah became fiercely aware of his closeness. She could feel her skin heat. Heavens, with her seated and him standing so near, she was at eye level with his...his middle section.

She flicked a hurried glance to his handsome profile. Didn't it bother him to stand so close to her? Didn't he feel even a portion of the simmering tingles that she'd come to expect when they were near each other? And what about their kisses? Didn't the memory of their passionate kissing linger in his thoughts?

Sarah looked from him to the drawings that held his attention. Apparently not. She stifled the impulse to jump to her feet, roll the sketches into a heap and then set fire to them.

Crazy. This mild-mannered man with the features and body of a warrior was driving her crazy. Sarah pulled her bottom lip between her teeth. She was getting as bad as Julie. And oh, dear, that reminded her. She hadn't gotten around to telling Lucas that he was going to have an encounter with a midnight visitor who had seduction on her mind. Sarah had discovered such an announcement was difficult to work into casual conversation.

"Are the disabled children going to be able to ride?"

Lucas's question forced her to return her attention to the drawings. "Actually the main reason we want to feature horseback riding is for the disabled."

"Why is that?"

"Because riding a horse and feeling its rhythmic sway is a lot like walking. The horses will give the kids more freedom than most of them have ever experienced."

"I see what you mean—they'll be able to explore the area surrounding the lake without any physical limitations."

"Exactly—the horses will make them . . . less different from the other children."

Sarah watched, fascinated when Lucas moved his tanned hand to where the remodeled motel units were located. He had held her with that hand, touched her, caressed her. She swallowed.

"And you're planning on having both boys and girls at the same camp—isn't that unusual?"

"Ye-yes." She cleared her throat. "But Camp Grey Horse is going to cater to children between the ages of five and twelve. There shouldn't be any complications of the...er...boy/girl variety."

"No kissing behind the stables, hmm?"

Not unless I can talk you into meeting me there.... "Uh, no, I don't think we'll have any problems like that."

Lucas straightened, but didn't move away. "It looks great, Sarah. All of it. Do you accept contributions?"

Sarah looked up at him in surprise. "Why?"

"I think you've got a worthwhile idea here, something to make life more meaningful for dozens of kids. I'd like to contribute."

"But we're a profit-making business—at least we will be in a couple of years. I don't think the I.R.S. approves of taxpayers donating money to noncharitable organizations."

While considering the drawings, Lucas stuck his hands into his trouser pockets and slowly rocked back and forth. Sarah tried mightily not to let Lucas's lean-hipped body sidetrack her thoughts.

"You're right of course. But I still want to help. I'd like to know that something I did, something Rockworth Construction did, played a part in making your camp a reality."

"Lucas, do you realize how special you are?" She scooted back her chair and stood. Maybe meeting him on a more even footing would snap her wayward awareness of him.

A flush swept Lucas's features. Taking a breath, Sarah continued. "I *was* wondering if your architect could take a look at our plans. And when your construction crew shows up to remodel your cabin, maybe we could arrange for them to do the work on Camp Grey Horse, too."

Lucas raised his brows. "Had it all figured out, did you?"

She smiled innocently. "You own a construction company, Lucas. We need some constructing done. What could be more natural than us working together?"

"And if I hadn't come along?"

"I would have fallen into a heap on the sand and probably become bear brunch."

He shook his head. "No way. You would have made a dive for the lake and outswum Mamma Bear to the other side."

Sarah laughed. "That was Plan B."

At the mention of that particular term, Sarah's laughter subsided. She looked at the kitchen clock and realized that right this minute Julie was probably planning her seduction of Lucas.

"I'm glad I was there to catch you, Sarah."

The deep pitch of his voice and the darkening of his gaze again chased away all thoughts of Lucas's niece. "Me, too," she whispered.

"And I'm glad Rockworth Construction is going to help build Camp Grey Horse."

Sarah blinked, trying to free herself from his mesmerizing stare. This was business they were discussing. She needed all of her faculties. "We'll need a bid from you, to make sure we can afford your services."

Lucas moved closer, and Sarah retreated a step. Tansy and Ben had gone to bed hours ago. Julie was upstairs—probably primping her heart out. And she, Sarah Burke, was alone with the most appealing man she'd ever met. And even though she knew he was generally reserved, she found herself very susceptible to this newly assertive Lucas.

And what of her lofty plans for celibacy and a heart-secure life? She planned to live that life alone and independent. She sighed, realizing that planning was what a person did until the living got in the way.

If Lucas could overcome his shyness to reach out to her, then couldn't she overcome her fears and insecurities about loving again? Lucas continued to move toward her.

"A bid, hmmm?" He stared down at her with thoughtful intensity.

"I was going to contact a local architect and several contractors in Sandpoint. I would have taken several competing bids for the work."

"Very practical."

"I can be." *When I'm not being stalked by a man who has a look of endless hunger in his eyes.*

"You'll have my bid."

"Well...uh...good night then." *Coward, Sarah. You're a coward.*

Lucas had backed her up against a wall with his head tipped toward her. "Not yet."

"Not yet?"

His low laugh crept along the nerve endings of her spine and somehow lodged in the pit of her stomach. "Why, Sarah, are you repeating me?"

The tip of her tongue moistened her lips. "Lucas, the suspense is killing me. Are you, or aren't you going to kiss me?"

His dark eyes glittered. "What do you think?"

"I think you've gotten over your shyness quicker than I've gotten over my..." Her words dwindled. Sarah found it impossible to speak the word while gazing into his passionate stare.

"Celibacy?"

She nodded.

He smiled. "That was for other men."

"Oh."

His strong hands settled at her shoulders. "Not for me."

She couldn't refute him.

"Come here, Sarah." He pulled her into his embrace.

I'm here! Oh, dear, I most certainly am...here... His kiss was both gentle and demanding. It spoke a language more primitive, more intimate than words. Lucas used his tongue to part her lips. He was inside her. First delicately, then deeply—inside her.

She shuddered against him. It was as if her entire body were dissolving into tiny particles of electrical energy. Then somehow the particles rejoined, and she was again whole. But different. Her hands came up around his neck, and she held on to Lucas for dear life.

This magic business was serious stuff. He had the power to take her apart and put her together again. Only now there seemed to be more of her—new parts.

Parts that throbbed and tingled and burned and...ached. Oh, dear Lord, she did ache for him—in all the new places he'd fashioned inside her.

For him. Despite her innocence, she knew those special places were for him to fill. Just Lucas. This dear, tender man of her dreams. Strange that a woman could dream about a man when she hadn't really believed he existed.

Her fingertips sank into the silky hair that grew at his nape. She pressed as close to him as she could get without crawling inside his clothing. She could hear the tiny moans she was making as Lucas's fingers pressed into her bottom and held her against his rigid desire. Nothing she'd ever experienced before with a man had been this...this real.

Where were they going? What special place was Lucas taking her to? Oh, she knew what usually happened between a man and woman when they came together physically. But this was more than that. It had to be. There was some mysterious fulfillment her body sought that surely couldn't be satisfied by the biological alignment of their separate parts.

His hungry kisses, his intimate caresses, his husky murmurs.... They all must lead to a place beyond physical coupling. The whole had to be greater than the sum of the parts. And she craved to discover for herself where the magic was taking them. She pressed closer.

"Oh, darling, you're so sweet. You taste so good..."

His hot, whispery words trailed off, and his mouth tenderly feasted on the sensitive column of her throat. Despite the heat, or perhaps because of it, she shivered. Then, because his faintly stubbled jaw tempted her, she tasted him.

She felt Lucas shudder in reaction to her boldness. His fingers gripped her tighter. Inadvertently he squeezed the tender area where she'd been stung, and Sarah cried out.

Lucas's head snapped up, his dark eyes flashing his concern. "Did I hurt you?"

She reached down to loosen his painful grip. "It's my sting," she explained, a blush stealing across her cheeks.

Lucas stared down at her blankly. In his aroused state, her words were incomprehensible to him. "What?"

"My bee sting. You remember..."

Understanding flooded his features. "Yes, of course I remember." He shook his head, clearly having difficulty getting his bearings.

His confusion thrilled Sarah. It was wonderful to know Lucas had been as shaken as she by the passionate interlude.

"Maybe we better say good-night," Sarah suggested softly, needing time to come to terms with her yearning for Lucas.

"We've already said good-night, honey. It didn't stop us from wanting each other then. And it needn't stop us now. Come to my room with me."

Sarah's eyes became huge. "Just like that?"

Lucas frowned at her stunned reaction to his suggestion. Couldn't she see that they belonged together? Wasn't she feeling the same desire that was quickly tearing him apart? There was only one way tonight could end. With them together. In bed—his bed.

"When you respond to a man the way you were, Sarah. There can be only one result."

Sarah ran a trembling hand through her hair. "I wouldn't know about that. *You're* the only man I've ever...er...responded to like...that." She waved her hand between them.

"Take my word for it. What we were doing leads in only one direction."

She stared into his eyes, confused by his sudden confident manner. This bold man talking so casually about making love bore little resemblance to her tenderhearted Lucas.

"Bu-but, Lucas. Surely you can see we're moving too fast. We've only just met. I know you aren't the kind of man to jump into an affair with a stranger. You're much too sensitive, too—"

"Oh, my God."

Lucas's moan made Sarah jump. "What is it? What's wrong?"

I forgot...forgot you've built me up in your mind as some kind of fantasy Mr. Nice Guy.

Lucas swore to himself. In the space of a few searing moments, he'd forgotten Sarah's mistaken impressions of him. Forgotten she was inexperienced while he was more than a little jaded. Forgotten the most important thing of all—Sarah Burke wasn't made for casual loving.

But, dear Lord, the softness of her body, the honeyed taste of her mouth and her obvious desire for him had given him a major case of amnesia. He felt like scum. He'd deceived her about the kind of man he was, grabbed at her like an oversexed teenager and...and demanded that she hop into bed with him. He was worse than scum.

"Lucas, what's wrong?"

"I . . ." He cleared his throat. "I . . ." Somewhere there had to be the words inside him that could get him out of his predicament. He'd start by telling her that he really wasn't all that . . . nice.

Lord, after tonight he'd never use that word again. He was heartily sick of it. He might just go out and find a dog to kick so he could prove to himself and Sarah that he and *nice* were like honky-tonk and opera—diametrically opposed.

Sarah's eyes filled with compassion. Poor Lucas really was shaken up by what had happened between them. She put her hand on his arm. "It's all right, Lucas. I know what you're trying to say."

He considered her melting golden brown eyes. "Somehow I don't think you do."

She smiled softly. "It caught us both by surprise, didn't it? You weren't any more prepared than I to cope with this strong attraction between us."

"No, I don't suppose I was."

"I'm proud of you, Lucas."

"Oh, honey. I really think you need to listen to what I've got to say."

"But I know what you're going to say."

He bit back a groan. "Do you?"

"You're going to apologize for coming on too strong, right?"

He squirmed under her warm gaze. "Well, actually—"

"And you're going to tell me how difficult it was for you to overcome your shyness and invite me to your bedroom."

"Sarah, you really don't—"

"And that's why I'm so proud of you."

"What?"

"For overcoming your inhibitions. It's a wonderful feeling for me to know that I have that effect on you. I wonder if you realize how much braver you are than I."

"Oh, honey, this has got to stop. I can't go on with you thinking—"

She rendered him speechless by throwing herself into his arms. "Don't you understand? I need to find the same courage you found. I need to let go of the past, let go of my fears of getting hurt. And you, you wonderful man, have shown me that I can."

Feeling helpless, Lucas's arms came around Sarah. Lord, she was incredible. She could only see the best in a person. He didn't want to let her down, to disillusion her.

When he'd kissed her in the meadow, he'd toyed with the idea of pretending to be the man she believed him to be. Then his doubts about himself and what he could offer a caring woman such as Sarah had made him realize he couldn't take advantage of her. But holding her now, he wondered if he could change.

Maybe he could turn out to be a different man than his father. A man worthy of Sarah.

"Sarah, we need to talk."

She loosened her embrace and smiled up at him. "I know. And we need to take things slower between us. It's great that you're overcoming your shyness with women, but we shouldn't rush things." She found his blush enchanting. Dear, sweet man.

He rubbed his palms slowly along her sleeves. "You're right about me needing to apologize to you. I had no business trying to hustle you off to bed. My attraction to you did catch me by surprise."

"Then shall we take things slower? Spend time getting to know each other?"

If I take about twenty cold showers a day, we might stand a chance of a slow courtship. "Can't think of anything I'd rather do. Come on, I'll walk you to your room."

Sarah took three steps toward the kitchen door, then stopped abruptly. "Uh, Lucas, there's something I forgot to tell you."

"Why do I have the feeling I'm not going to like hearing this?"

She smiled brightly at him. "There's a slight problem you've got to take care of before you can go to bed."

"And what's that?"

"Julie. She's waiting for you."

Lucas's eyes narrowed. "Where?"

"In your room." The words were as small as she could make them.

"Why?"

"To seduce you."

"What?"

"Now, Lucas. It wasn't my fault. I was just trying to razzle-dazzle her with some fancy footwork, and she kind of misunderstood what I was saying. She thought I was challenging her to see which of us could seduce you first. But what I meant was—"

"Sarah." His hands gripped her shoulders, and he shook her gently. "I can't go upstairs and talk to Julie in my bedroom."

"I know. I've been racking my brain all afternoon to think of something that would get you off the hook."

He shook her again. "Try harder."

"The thing is, Julie's past the point of listening to reason. She thinks she's in love with you."

"Then I'm just going to have to set her straight. But the minute I do, she's going to be on her way to Hawaii."

"The problem with Julie is she's at the age where she thinks she can 'convince' you to love her."

Lucas ran a hand through his hair. "I thought you were going to fix that?"

"I tried! But Julie is determined to make you return her love."

"Baloney."

"It has to do with romance, Lucas. To a fourteen-year-old girl, there's nothing more romantic than having an older man in love with her. Even if you came out and told her that you could never love her, she wouldn't believe you."

Suddenly Lucas's gaze sharpened. "Unless..."

"Unless what?" Sarah asked, uneasy at his fierce expression.

"I was in love with someone else."

"According to you, if she believed that, she'd call her father."

Lucas swore again. "Then there's no way out."

"You'll have to let her down easily—in stages."

"How do I do that?"

Sarah searched her mind for a solution to Lucas's dilemma. There had to be an answer. What line of reasoning would appeal to an overly romantic fourteen-year-old girl? Sarah thought about Deborah's teenage daughter. Being in a wheelchair, Wendy did a lot of reading. Recently she'd become fascinated by the story of Cyrano de Bergerac.

Suddenly Sarah grinned. "I've got it, Lucas."

He stared at her warily. "Got what?"

"The solution to our problem."

His features brightened. "Great, what's the answer?"

"Poetry."

"Ah, Sarah, do you want to expand on that?" He no longer looked quite so hopeful.

"It's simple. You can do what Cyrano de Bergerac did."

"Wasn't he a sword fighter? Somehow I don't think—"

"Listen, this is going to work. Before you go up to your room tonight, you need to write a couple of pages of poetry—some really gushy stuff."

"Assuming that I can do that, how's it going to help?"

"The poetry will be about me. When Julie comes into your room, just start reading it. There's no way she can make a pass at you while you're reading love lyrics about another woman. Trust me."

"Does it matter that I don't know how to write poetry?"

Sarah guided him back to the table and thrust a pen into his hand while she reached for a blank sheet of paper. "Do you want to cure Julie's crush on you?"

His eyebrows drawn together, Lucas stared at the paper. "Poetry...rhymes, doesn't it?"

"Most of the time."

"I could be here all night!"

"Then that will solve your problem with Julie." Sarah decided this was an opportune time to leave. "I think I'll run up to bed now. I'm exhausted. See you in the morning, Lucas."

He looked up from the empty page. "You bet you will."

"Good morning, Sarah."

Lucas's low-voiced greeting reached Sarah as she picked up a crisp slice of bacon. Looking up from the table, she encountered his formidable expression. No gentleness lurked within the hard-planed contours of his face. No light sparkled in his dark eyes, and no smile softened the firm line of his mouth. Lucas Rockworth did not look like a man who'd spent a restful night.

"Good morning, Lucas." Sarah let her gaze drift away from him and return to her plate.

After Tansy had dished breakfast onto heated serving plates, she and her little boy had gone outside. Without Julie's presence, there was no buffer between Sarah and Lucas's dark mood. She was reluctant to inquire how the impromptu poetry reading had gone.

Lucas pulled out a chair next to her and claimed it. Sliding another quick glance at his somber face, she noted that his gloomy state in no way diminished his handsomeness. The light blue shirt he wore did wonderful things to his broad chest, and his dark slacks accentuated his muscular legs. It wouldn't do to sigh at his ruggedly attractive appearance, but the sigh was there, inside her, just waiting to slip out.

Lucas didn't break the silence, and Sarah wasn't inclined to rush in and fill it. Instead she methodically pushed the food around on her plate, making interesting geometric configurations from the scrambled eggs and hash browns.

Lucas just as methodically ate everything he'd served himself. When he was finished eating, he drained his tumbler of orange juice and reached for his napkin. Then he pushed back his chair, obviously about to leave the kitchen.

Sarah cracked. "All right, Lucas. It couldn't have been *that* bad. What happened?"

He looked down at her with a martyred expression, opened his mouth, then closed it. He shook his head twice and walked away from the table. Sarah jumped to her feet.

"Lucas, wait. You've got to tell me what happened." She put a hand on his forearm to stop him from leaving.

He glanced down at her restraining hand, then into her eyes.

"My ladylove is Sarah.
She was almost devoured by a 'bear-ah.'
Then she fell into my arms and
I sampled her charms.
Now I live to make her mine,
for all time."

Sarah's mouth fell open at Lucas's deadpan recitation. The poetry was too awful to be real. Except for the last line. That last line wasn't half bad.

"Well?"

She jumped at his terse question. "That's really nice, Lucas."

He cringed at her use of the word he fully intended to eradicate from his vocabulary. "Three hours, Sarah. It took me three hours and about a hundred sheets of paper to come up with that."

He stepped closer, and Sarah snatched her hand from his arm. "Well, you hung in there until you finished. That's what's important. How did...uh...Julie react to it?"

"By the time I got to my room, she had fallen asleep—in my bed. When I was walking past your room, I debated waking you to give you a progress report. But I decided to let you enjoy your undeserved sleep."

"That was ni—"

"Don't say it."

"What?" Sarah squeaked, more than a little awed at Lucas's demonstration of anger.

"Nice. You were going to say 'nice,' weren't you?"

Eyes wide, she nodded.

"Don't."

"O-okay."

He sighed hugely. "Thank you."

"You're welcome."

"Come on. Let's go." He took her arm and led her toward the back door.

"Where?"

"To the future site of Camp Grey Horse. I want to go over your plans with you before the architect shows up."

Sarah found herself taking two steps to each one of his. "What's the hurry?"

"I want to get out of here before Julie comes downstairs."

"Oh."

"And I need your help on this poetry business. I want to be able to rattle off six or seven love poems to Julie. That ought to discourage her."

"But I'm no poet," Sarah protested.

Lucas dropped her arm and turned to face her. He was smiling, a thoroughly nasty smile. "But you're going to hang in there till you come up with something—right?"

Sarah studied his militant expression. Boy had he woken up on the wrong side of the bed!

"How do I love thee? Let me count the—"

"It's been done, Sarah." A smile threatened the severe line of his mouth.

"Well, then, how about:

Rose are red
violets are blue
Sarah Burke is as beautiful as . . ."

". . . Timbuktu?" Lucas filled in, smothering a chuckle.

Dark brown eyes met golden brown. Laughter shone in both. "We'll work on it," they promised in unison.

Chapter Seven

Sarah."

Lucas's deep voice weaved its way into Sarah's dreams. Sighing softly, she turned sleepily in its direction.

"Time to wake up. Your business partner's arrived." A smile touched his lips. Sarah was wearing her red long johns.

The days since he'd plucked Sarah Burke from the sky had been the richest and happiest of his life. They had spent practically every waking moment together. Naturally he'd been on his best behavior. No impulsive kisses, no more midnight swims, and *no* side trips into her bedroom.

Until now.

His week with Sarah was up. Deborah Scott was downstairs, all proprietary and concerned at finding the note tacked on a bungalow door, informing her of Sarah's whereabouts.

It wasn't enough.

He wanted more. More time. More Sarah.

He stared down at her. She was all warm and flushed from sleep. What he wanted was the right to take off his clothes and climb into that bed with her.

Lucas reached out and smoothed back a sable strand of hair that had fallen across her cheek. She had taught him more about himself in a week than he'd learned in a lifetime. She'd taught him that the joy and zest for life were inside him—just waiting for her arrival to set them free. To set him free.

And she'd taught him that he needn't end up like his father.

He wanted her. Passionately. Irrevocably. And he was convinced she wanted him. Oh, she still had stars in her eyes about his basic temperament. But no man could be as wholesome as she thought him to be.

He'd tried to live up to her illusions about him and in the process shocked a few of his business associates with his new telephone personality. His smile widened as he recalled inquiring after his secretary's newest grandchild, his vice president's vacation plans off the China coast and his architect's new bride. They'd all reacted with varying degrees of shock. But they had answered. And he'd learned some important things about the people he worked with. Thanks to Sarah.

"Sarah, come on. Deborah Scott's waiting downstairs with a look of mistrust in her big gray eyes."

"Lucas..." They were alone together. In a dark, secret place. He was touching her. Everywhere. It felt wonderful.... She wanted to touch him, too. But Deborah was there, pulling them apart. And suddenly Ryan was also there. "Leave us alone...."

Lucas chuckled softly. "I've heard of the royal 'we'—was that a royal 'us'?"

Sarah's eyelids drifted open. Lucas's dark gaze imprisoned her. She felt a flutter deep inside her. Instinctively she reached for him.

Lucas felt Sarah's hands on his shoulders and groaned. Oh, Lord, it wasn't doing his self-control any good to discover Sarah Burke woke up...ready. The same way he'd awakened every morning this week. He leaned across her, unable to resist taking one sweet kiss.

The kiss *was* sweet. But there was nothing chaste about it. His mouth hungered for her as desperately as the rest of him. And she yielded without restraint.

Still disoriented from sleep, Sarah surrendered to the waves of sensual excitement that flooded through her. When Lucas's hands released her buttons, she moved urgently beneath the blankets that held her trapped.

Lucas's hands found their way past the parted material, to the sensitive skin beneath. Hot tremors of desire cascaded through her. Never before had she hurt from pleasure. But she did now. The pleasure was unspeakably delicious, but the hurting went on and on. She needed Lucas to make the hurting go away. And to make it go away, he needed to fill her.

"Please," she breathed against his lips.

"Sarah..." It was a groan ripped from his soul. He wanted her more than the breath he was gulping into his bursting lungs. But he couldn't take her. Not like this. Not when he'd given her no chance to make a rational decision.

Clamping down a control he'd never suspected he possessed, Lucas pulled away from her. Quickly, before he could change his mind, he rebuttoned her top.

And if someone had dared tell him that only a nice man would do something so noble, he would have socked him. Twice.

Suddenly completely awake, Sarah stared into Lucas's flushed face. She had no idea why he had come into her bedroom. Nor was she sure which part of what she'd experienced was dream, which part reality. A hasty glance at the front of her longjohns revealed the peaks of her breasts pressing against red fabric.

She jerked her gaze back to Lucas's sharpened features. He was breathing hard, as if he'd run a great distance. As she gazed into Lucas's stormy eyes, she comprehended that the vision of his tanned fingers against her bare flesh was the stuff of reality—not dreamland.

And?

And the single burning question in her mind was why had he stopped?

"Deborah Scott's waiting downstairs for you."

"Wh-when did she get here?" Sarah asked shakily.

He met her turbulent gaze head-on. "Half hour ago."

Sarah placed a trembling hand to her pounding heart. "Then I'd better hurry."

"I don't want you to leave."

Sarah held his dark stare, wondering if she'd heard him correctly. After what had just happened, how could she stay? Unless he'd decided to... finish what he'd begun. She was stunned to realize how much she wanted him to. Finish. To take her once and for all to that magic place of fulfillment.

They'd spent a week together. Laughing, talking, planning—walking along mountain paths, coming to better know each other. She felt dangerously close to being in love with him. Did Lucas feel those same heady emotions toward her? It was impossible to know. He kept his feelings bottled up inside himself.

She shook her head slowly, focusing on the present. What was growing between herself and Lucas wouldn't be resolved in the next few minutes.

"Lucas, Deborah's waiting for me."

"There's room for her. She can stay, too."

"Deborah was planning on bringing her daughter with her," Sarah protested faintly. The determination filling Lucas's dark eyes seemed at odds with his mild personality.

"I met Wendy. There's room for her—for all of you. Please stay with me, Sarah."

She sensed how difficult it was for Lucas to voice such a strong plea. "I'll talk to Deborah. She wasn't too excited about living in a tent while we got Camp Grey Horse in working order."

"I'll go down and keep her company while you get dressed. Julie's already getting acquainted with Wendy."

Sarah sat up, pushing the blankets back. "Wendy's a year older than Julie."

"When Julie discovered that Wendy was in a wheelchair, Julie seemed to grow up a bit. See you downstairs."

Sarah nodded absently, her mind suddenly preoccupied with what Deborah must have thought when she'd discovered her business partner was living with a man. Somehow this time with Lucas had seemed unrelated to the rest of her life, as if it were separate from everything that had gone before. Separate from the rules of everyday living. With Deborah's arrival, Sarah was reminded that the rules still applied.

Leaning casually against the kitchen counter, Lucas slowly sipped the coffee Tansy had given him before she'd gone outside to see if Julie and Wendy wanted breakfast served on the sun deck. Through the kitchen window, he saw Tansy's son homesteading a corner of the deck, surrounded by a miniature army of plastic space invaders.

Deborah Scott sat at the table, cradling a mug of steaming coffee. He noticed Ms. Scott's hands trembled. The tension gripping her pale features made her look older than he guessed her to be. And yet the faint lines in no way diminished her loveliness.

He rubbed his thumb across the rim of his cup. The last time he'd seen Ms. Scott had been at his office when she'd shown up to tell him she wasn't going to sell him her mountain property. He'd been furious. She'd picked a particularly rotten time to appear. Moments earlier he'd been informed by his father that Rockworth had been underbid on a multimillion-dollar project that they'd assumed was in the bag.

It had only been after Deborah Scott had left his office that he'd realized it had taken a great deal of class, not to mention courage, to face him in person with her news. She could have had her broker contact him, or she could have called him on the phone. He hadn't seen her since that stormy encounter.

She'd aged five years. Faint shadows bruised the pale flesh beneath her bluish-gray eyes. Tiny furrows bracketed her soft mouth, and her movements had a jerkiness that suggested Deborah Scott was living on nerves, the fine cutting edge of those nerves.

Again he glanced out the window that overlooked the sun deck. Wendy was speaking earnestly to Julie and Tansy. His gaze returned to Ms. Scott, who stared broodingly into her coffee. Being widowed and having a teenage daughter in a wheelchair had to be stressful. He wondered if Sarah's business partner was up to handling the demands of running Camp Grey Horse.

A movement of yellow at the kitchen entry swung his gaze to a glowing Sarah. She came into the kitchen laughing.

"Deborah! You found me!" Arms extended, she rushed across the room to her friend and pulled Deborah Scott from her chair. Sarah hugged her tightly.

Lucas couldn't help contrasting their appearances. Deborah wore a long-sleeved Oxford shirt neatly tucked into gray linen slacks. The outfit accented Ms. Scott's tall and very slender frame. Sarah wore white jeans and her butter-colored sweatshirt. Deborah's ebony-colored hair was stylishly cut while Sarah's dark hair fell in a silken swath to her shoulders.

Sarah was soft and warm, like sunshine splashing across a spring meadow. Deborah was fragile as if stiffly held together by a composure Lucas suspected went only skin deep.

The women stepped apart. Lucas noticed that Deborah had clung to Sarah a little longer and a little more tightly than Sarah had to her.

"Of course, I found you. This is the only cabin on the lake that's next to our property and currently occupied."

Sarah smiled widely. "Thank heavens for that." She turned to Lucas. "This man not only saved me from a very pushy bear, Deborah. But after said bear trashed my campsite, Lucas offered me a place to stay for the week. I know you two have already met."

Lucas nodded to Deborah. He saw her step protectively closer to Sarah. "Yes, I remember Mr. Rockworth."

Lucas tried a disarming smile on the obviously hostile woman. "It's a little late, but I'd like to apologize for my behavior at our last meeting. I'm afraid I didn't react very graciously to your decision to keep your property."

Deborah Scott raised her eyebrows. "Your strong language on the subject made that patently clear, Mr. Rockworth."

Almost immediately, Sarah began to realize that her best friend and the man she was ten minutes away from falling in love with were not . . . compatible. Deborah's reference to Lucas's use of "strong" language showed Sarah what a mistaken impression her friend must have gained of the real Lucas.

"Deborah, you've got to realize how much your decision not to go through with the sale of your property disturbed Lucas's plans."

Sarah felt herself drawn to Lucas's side and crossed the room to stand next to him. When his arm came across her shoulders, she leaned against him. At that moment their being together felt very right.

"As I remember when I left . . . 'Lucas's' office, the words of a threatened lawsuit were ringing in my ears."

Tipping her head back, Sarah saw Lucas's flushed face. Poor guy. That was probably the only time in his life he had been assertive, and it was coming back to haunt him. Sarah straightened under the comforting weight of his arm. She was fully prepared to champion this gentle man—even against her best friend.

"Lucas has already apologized for what happened in his office, Deborah. He was under a lot of pressure. His doctor had practically ordered him to find a quiet place to relax, or risk having a heart attack." Sarah knew she was exaggerating, but she didn't care. Deborah needed to understand how much the lakeside property had meant to Lucas.

"Apology accepted then."

"Thank you." Lucas harbored no illusions that Sarah's friend was warming up to him. "I mentioned to Sarah that you and your daughter are welcome to stay here with her, while you get Camp Grey Horse off the ground."

"How generous." A brittle smile claimed Deborah's mouth. "But I've been looking forward to camping out."

Sarah gazed at Deborah in amazement. When she'd dropped Sarah off a week ago, Deborah's last words had been that she was *not* looking forward to a month of roughing it while they remodeled the motel units and built the main lodge.

"It's going to be difficult for your daughter to live in a tent and get around in her wheelchair," Lucas observed, his tone neutral.

Deborah's face lost what little color it had. "I'm fully aware of the difficulties Wendy faces. I've already thanked you for helping me lift her wheelchair up the front steps of your cabin."

"I didn't—"

Deborah interrupted him. "Sarah's brother has placed his motor home at our disposal for as long as we need it. It is fully equipped."

"When did Ryan buy a motor home?" Sarah asked in surprise. "He's never been camping in his life."

Deborah turned to Sarah. "It's new. Evidently he came across it when a prospective buyer wanted to use it as a down payment on a home. The amazing thing is that it's been customized to accommodate a wheelchair."

Sarah had difficulty digesting Deborah's announcement. From the beginning, Ryan had been a hostile force regarding the development of Camp Gray Horse. "Ryan, *my* brother, is lending us a motor home?"

Deborah nodded, then directed a cool smile at Lucas. "So you see, Sarah, Wendy and I will get along just fine on our own, Mr. Rockworth."

Lucas "saw" that he was in danger of losing Sarah to the overprotective and antagonistic influence of Deborah Scott.

"Though perhaps there is one thing you can help us with, Mr. Rockworth."

"And what's that?" he inquired warily.

"Sarah needs to check in with her brother. I assume you have a telephone?"

"In the den," he acknowledged.

With exasperated indulgence Sarah had watched the cool byplay between two of the dearest people in her life. She was convinced it wouldn't take long for them to become friends. But in the interim life was going to be very...interesting.

"I guess I should call Ryan." She moved to the entry, then paused for a moment. "By the way, Deborah, I've decided to use Lucas's architect for Camp Grey Horse's final designs. And Rockworth will probably be doing the construction for us."

* * *

Several hours later, Lucas was whistling as he came up the path that led from the lake to his cabin. His dark mood at having Sarah move out of his cabin had lightened.

She was still going to be at the lake, and they would be spending a great deal of time together, working on her designs, deciding what kind of materials she was going to use and overseeing the actual building. And, without her being one thin bedroom wall away from him each night, it was going to be easier for him to get a decent night's sleep.

He still hadn't worked his way past the fact that Sarah deserved a loving commitment from the man who would claim her first, last and always. He knew he wanted her, of course. Oh, Lord, did he know that. But what filled the space between wanting and... loving? He needed to know that answer before he and Sarah took their ultimate journey together.

And he had to let her know he wasn't the knight in shining armor she'd convinced herself he was—convinced herself with some help from him, he admitted. But with Deborah Scott's arrival, it was unlikely Sarah would continue to look at him with eyes of tender admiration.

Lucas climbed the back steps to the cabin. He'd just come from pushing Wendy's wheelchair down the path that led to the boat dock. Tansy had assisted Julie. He grinned, recalling Ben's plastic bucket overflowing with creepy little aliens. It had been an odd assortment, Julie, Wendy, Tansy and Ben. But the prospects of some summer sun, Tansy's picnic lunch and Julie's portable tape player had formed the cohesive elements to make a pleasant afternoon for the group.

He opened the back door and walked toward the kitchen where he heard Deborah's and Sarah's laughter. When he reached the entry, he stood there silently, unable to believe his eyes.

Deborah Scott was giggling like a schoolgirl. Gone were the lines of stress. Her beautiful face was relaxed and filled with a happy serenity. Even the dark smudges beneath her eyes seemed to have faded.

He shifted his gaze to Sarah. Her head was tipped back, and she, too, was giggling, and talking *and* gesturing with a crispy chicken drumstick.

"It's true! The dumb bee got me on my bottom. You should have seen him. He was huge!"

"Oh, Sarah, I'm sorry for laughing, but just the thought of Lucas Rockworth being pursued by a bumblebee is hysterical."

Sarah's face sobered. "It could have been a disaster."

"Why's that?" Deborah wiped her eyes with the back of her hand.

"Lucas is allergic to bee venom, and he didn't have his antitoxin with him."

"I don't believe it. Lucas Rockworth allergic to bees." She shook her head.

Lucas walked into the kitchen and savored the special warmth that seemed to flow from Sarah. She looked up just as she took a healthy bite from the meaty drumstick.

It hit him in that highly unromantic moment how much he'd come to care for Sarah. That knowledge made him more than a little nervous—considering she still thought of him as a very meek man. What would she do when she discovered the truth, that his basic nature was less lamb than... lion...?

Sarah pounded another red-handkerchiefed stake into the soft dirt, then stood. She laid aside the hammer she'd been using and flexed her fingers. "I think I'm getting a blister."

A few feet away, Deborah looked up from the correspondence she'd been shifting through. They'd set up a card table under the shade of three towering pines.

"I wish you'd let me help you with that, Sarah. I'm feeling guilty just sitting on my bottom, while you're sweating like a horse."

"I take exception to that." Sarah took a moment to stretch the kinks from her body before she moved into the shade and claimed the chair next to Deborah. "I prefer to think I sweat like a prima ballerina—with great profusion, you understand—but *femininely*."

Sarah poured herself a glass of lemonade from the half-filled pitcher and sat back in her chair. She had known Deborah for more than eight years. When she'd been a college student at Washington State, she had lived with Deborah and her husband.

Dorms and off-campus housing had not been deemed suitable living accommodations by her overprotective older brother. But Ryan had approved of her living in the home of his best friend—a family man. Ryan's best friend was Deborah's late husband. Sarah had come to despise her brother's friend, but she'd come to think of Deborah as the older sister she'd never had.

Gradually Sarah became aware of Deborah's silence. "Why so quiet? Aren't we going to meet our quota of campers for July and August?"

Deborah looked up from the applications she'd been reviewing. "Our only problem is limiting the number of children we can accept. We already have more than a hundred applicants for next year's season."

Sarah held the chilled glass to her perspiring forehead. "You've done a fantastic job promoting Camp Grey Horse. Don't worry about how little it looks like Lucas and I've accomplished so far in getting the darn thing built."

Deborah surveyed the string-connected, red-flagged stakes that marked the clearing. "It's hard to believe it's going to be finished in less than two months."

Sarah took another sip of her lemonade, then sighed. "Well, it will be. Lucas's architect has completed the plans, and his work crew will be here next week."

"Isn't it amazing how much lower his bid was than any of the local contractors in Sandpoint?"

A pleased smile settled across Sarah's mouth. "Not so amazing. He wanted to contribute to Camp Grey Horse, and his way of doing that was not to make a profit on the job."

"Your Lucas Rockworth is full of surprises. From our brief meeting in his office, I never would have pegged him as a Good Samaritan."

"That's because you don't know the real Lucas," Sarah confided, warming to her favorite subject. "Haven't you noticed how considerate he is? How he's made sure Wendy has access to the activities around the lake?"

"He's a remarkable man," Deborah agreed. "I appreciate him driving into Sandpoint and getting the materials to build the wheelchair ramps for Wendy. I hadn't expected him to be so...generous."

"I wish Ryan shared your opinion of Lucas. When he found out that I stayed with Lucas for an entire week, my brother practically fried the telephone wires between Spokane and Lucas's cabin."

Deborah smiled sympathetically. "Somehow that doesn't surprise me. Your older brother is very protective where you're concerned, Sarah."

"I know. I keep telling myself that's why he's so opposed to us working together to make Camp Grey Horse a reality. He's worried we might fail."

Deborah made no comment, and Sarah continued. "That's why I can't figure out why he loaned us a thirty-six-foot motor home. It doesn't make any sense."

"I guess he thinks if you're going to fail, you might as well do it in comfort."

"Men! Who can figure them?"

"Here comes Lucas. Spending the rest of the afternoon with him should give you an advanced course on the subject."

"Hello, ladies." Lucas looked from the crisply dressed Deborah Scott to the sweaty, dirt-smudged face of Sarah and grinned. Funny how he'd never noticed before that "earthy" women attracted him.

"Hi, Lucas, are the girls still working on their tans?"

"What?" He jerked his gaze from Sarah.

"The girls," Deborah prompted. "You know—my daughter and your niece."

"I brought back a couple of videos from Sandpoint. They're up to their pretty little ears in something called, *Dance Marathon*."

"Julie must be ecstatic at having her bandages off and being able to see again."

Deborah's voice was husky with emotion. Lucas and Sarah stared at each other, realizing how difficult it must be for Deborah to accept that there would be no similar cure for Wendy. Her daughter would never be free of her wheelchair.

"I think temporarily losing her sight helped Julie do some quick growing up," Lucas said gently. "I have to keep reminding myself Wendy's only fifteen. She's very mature for her age."

"The—the accident forced her to grow up." Deborah pushed back her chair and stood, her eyes shiny with unshed tears. "I think I'll wander over to the cabin and see how Wendy's doing."

Sarah and Lucas stared after the straight-backed woman as she followed the now well-worn path to Lucas's cabin. "I shouldn't have checked out that movie. I didn't think..." Lucas's deep voice trailed off.

"No, I think your choice of videos was good. There's a real world out there where boys and girls *do* dance. The sooner Wendy comes to terms with that world and tries to fit into it, the happier she'll be."

Lucas sat in the empty chair. "It's rough, though—and so damned unfair. She hasn't always been disabled, has she?"

Sarah shook her head. "Until a year ago, Wendy Scott was a perfectly ordinary girl. Deborah was separated from Wendy's father. One night he picked Wendy up to take her to a movie. Deborah hadn't realized he'd been drinking. I dropped by later that night to visit Deborah. When the doorbell rang, I answered it.''

Sarah swallowed and continued. ''There were two policemen at the door. Th-there had been a car accident. Wendy had been taken to the hospital. Her father had been killed on impact.''

''My God, how terrible.'' Lucas reached out and took her hands into his.

''Oh, it was terrible all right. Most of all for Deborah. She—she had a breakdown.''

''Oh, honey.'' He stood and pulled her into his arms.

Sarah wept softly against his chest. ''For two weeks we didn't know if Wendy was going to live, and Deborah was in shock.''

Lucas continued to comfort Sarah. He knew with unshakable conviction that it had been Sarah who'd pulled Deborah through the tragedy.

They embraced for several minutes. Gradually the remembered despair of Wendy's crippling accident lessened, and Sarah became aware of the scent of Lucas's woodsy after-shave. She rubbed her cheek against the smooth fabric of his shirt. Beneath it, she could feel the pounding of his heart. His hands tightened. Since Deborah had arrived at the lake, this was the first time he'd held her.

Sarah stood absolutely still, afraid to disturb the fragile intimacy of his embrace. His hands moved slowly across her back, then dropped lower. She inhaled sharply, still unmoving. After a few gentle caresses, his hands moved again to her back. She could feel his breath against the crown of her head.

"You feel so good, Sarah." He eased her from him, and his gaze swept her face.

Her hands rested lightly against his chest. Meeting her eyes, he reached out and cupped one breast. She mirrored his look of hunger, while the pressure of his shocking caress increased.

And despite the trees' shading, Sarah felt a slowly awakening heat fill her body. Deliberately he lessened the pressure, then used the pad of his thumb to massage the tip of her breast into throbbing rigidity. It didn't seem to matter that she wore both a T-shirt and bra.

"I want you more than I've wanted any other woman." The words were evenly spaced, carefully enunciated. His fingertips moved from her breast to her cheek. "We need time alone, Sarah. We need to understand what's happening between us. And...and we need to have a talk."

Talk? Surely they needed to do more than talk. During the past few weeks, Sarah had come to accept her attraction to Lucas Rockworth. Unfortunately, however, Lucas had reverted to his earlier shyness. Gone was the passionate man who'd insisted she join him in his bed.

It became clear to Sarah that, if this romance was going to progress to the next level of intimacy, she was going to have to take matters into her own hands. For Lucas's own good, she was to have to become the aggressor.

She smiled reassuringly at her nervous suitor. "Why don't we meet at the lake tonight and...talk?"

He stared at her intently, and Sarah was grateful he couldn't read her mind. This was one man who'd be better off *not* knowing that he was about to be swept off his feet.

"Okay, but I want you to promise that you'll listen to me with an open mind."

"Of course I will, Lucas. But you'll have to make that same promise to me."

"Consider it done." He glanced at his watch. "I told Julie I'd spend some time with her this afternoon. We better finish staking out the stables."

"Think you'll be safe, alone with her?"

"After all the poetry I've been reading about you?"

"Then our strategy is working?"

"You know, I really think it is."

Chapter Eight

I hate fishing—it's boring.''

Lucas looked at his disgruntled niece. Julie stood beside him on a wooden bridge that spanned a fast-moving stream. She held her fishing rod with lax fingers.

"You wanted to spend some time with me," he reminded her calmly.

"Fish stink."

"That's a succinct way of putting it. Tansy does know how to fry them up tasty, though."

"I guess so," Julie acknowledged in a disinterested tone. "How come you let Tansy dress like she does?"

Lucas released his fly reel and cast off again. The high-pitched sound of the uncurling line was strangely pleasing against the murmur of the stream.

"What's wrong with what Tansy wears?"

"Tank tops and shorts—that's no way for a cook and housekeeper to dress."

"What she wears doesn't affect how she does her job."

"Well, how come you let her bring Ben to the mountains? You even let Ben live with her at your house. That's not right."

Lucas slowly reeled in his line, squinting against its golden wake. "Not right to whom?"

"To people. They might get the wrong idea."

"No one who knows either Tansy or me would get the...wrong idea. She works for me, but we're also friends."

"Is she divorced?"

"I..." Lucas laid aside his pole and turned to Julie. "I'm not going to discuss Tansy's personal life with you."

"I'll bet she never even got married in the first place. I bet Ben's ille—"

"That's enough, Julie," Lucas said firmly. "Why are you suddenly so concerned about Tansy?"

"Everything about you concerns me. I thought you knew that. I don't want anyone taking advantage of your good nature."

"You think Tansy's taking advantage of me?"

"Well, she doesn't give you a solid eight-hour day. She spends a lot of time just gabbing—with Sarah."

So now we get to the real issue. "I don't have any complaints with Tansy's work or how she spends her time."

"What about how Sarah spends her time?" Julie persisted.

"What about it?"

"If Sarah's not keeping Tansy from doing her job, she's with you. She practically *smothers* you with attention."

"Sarah's special to me," Lucas said gently. "I care for her very much."

"More—more than me?" Julie's voice trembled.

"Not more, but differently."

"That's what my father said when he told me he was marrying your sister. Are—are you going to marry Sarah?"

"I read you some of the poems I've written about her."

"Making me laugh won't make me feel any better."

Sure it will. "Are you insulting my poetry?"

"Oh, Uncle Lucas." Julie laughed wobbly. "Your poetry's awful."

"Then help me write something better."

Julie nibbled her lower lip. "Don't you think you could wait for me to grow up before you...before you fall in love?"

Lucas felt his heart swell with affection for his niece. Whoever said growing up was hard to do had hit the nail on the head.

"I don't think so."

Julie raised her chin. "If it were the other way around, I'd wait."

"No, you wouldn't. Life just doesn't work that way."

"Then life stinks."

Lucas chuckled. "Yeah, sometimes it does. But most of the time life is pretty good."

"Maybe for grown-ups, but when you're a kid it's mostly taking orders."

He took it as a positive sign that Julie referred to herself as a kid.

"Being an adult means assuming responsibilities, Julie." He thought of his meeting tonight with Sarah at the lake. How was she going to react when he clued her in about his not-so-meek temperament?

"When I grow up, I'm going to be the boss. No one's going to tell me what to do."

Laughing, Lucas reached out and ruffled her hair. "When you hit twenty-five, I'll expect a progress report."

Julie wrinkled her brow. "When I'm twenty-five, you'll be..."

"Forty-six," Lucas filled in.

Her blue eyes widened. "No kidding? Gosh, my dad's forty, and he's *old*."

"Uses a cane, does he?"

"Well, no, but he's getting gray hair." She squinted up at him.

"Stop frowning, you'll be the only fourteen-year-old in America with wrinkles. Besides, I don't have any gray hair." He wondered it that would be true after tonight.

"Just checking. Uh, Uncle Lucas, thanks for calling Dad and asking if I could stay longer at the lake. Wendy would get awful lonely without me for company."

"You're getting to be good friends, aren't you?"

Julie nodded. "She's neat. I wish there was some way the doctors could fix it so she wouldn't have to stay in that wheelchair."

"Me, too, but it doesn't look like that's going to happen. And in the years to come, it's going to mean a lot to Wendy to have friends like you."

"She's already been a good friend to me. It—it helps to have someone your own age to talk to—about stuff."

"I guess it does at that." He reached for his pole. "What do you say we apply ourselves to some serious fishing?"

Standing in the motor home's miniscule shower with a head full of foaming shampoo running down her cheeks, Sarah planned her strategy for her upcoming rendezvous with Lucas. First, she would listen to whatever it was he had to tell her. Then she would casually put her hand on his arm and . . .

And what?

Vigorously Sarah rubbed her scalp.

And then . . . She'd kind of lean toward him, with her face tilted up so her mouth was just inches from his.

Sticking her head directly under the spraying water, she groped for her plastic bottle of conditioner.

Then she'd wait for him to kiss her.

She rinsed off the conditioner and turned off the shower.

But what if Lucas didn't close that short distance?

She reached for a towel and began to dry herself. How hard could it be to slip her arms around Lucas's neck and pull him toward her? Once they were kissing, she'd be able to rekindle the passion they'd experienced several weeks ago.

And where would this unbridled passion lead?

Sarah withdrew a pair of white panties from a drawer in the compact vanity.

To . . . to making love. . . .

Sarah thought about that for a minute. She was a virgin at age twenty-six, and now she was seriously thinking about making love to a man who wasn't her husband.

She slipped on a lacy white bra, then reached for her perfume. The scent of musk filled the tiny bathroom. Actually she'd been resisting the advances of men for about eight years.

And "men" could be narrowed down to...probably eight who had pressed for something more than a casual dating relationship. Eight years—eight men. Nice and tidy. Sarah took her white slacks from their hanger and pulled them over her hips.

Well, man number nine had come roaring into her life, and suddenly the status quo no longer applied. A frown drew her brows together. Something wasn't quite right, but she couldn't put her finger on it.

On the vanity next to her small makeup pouch was one of her favorite sweaters—a bulky, white cable knit with a wide cowl neck. She put it on, then plugged in Deborah's blow dryer and for a few moments thought of nothing.

Sarah was smoothing moisturizer over her skin and looking into the steamy mirror when she noticed the line marring her brow. Immediately she set her mind to understanding how it was possible for eight years of rational behavior to count for so little.

Talk about Lucas being nervous. *She* was the nervous one. Sarah stared at the tube of peach-colored lipstick held between her shaking fingers. Amend that. She was petrified. In the mirror she studied her too-huge eyes.

Panic-stricken?

Her reflection nodded back at her.

What are you doing, Sarah Burke? Do you really think you can seduce Lucas?

Sarah closed her eyes and tried to conjure his image. It came. Darkly handsome, fiercely masculine and . . . gentle. Loving. Tender. A tremor teased her stomach. She couldn't deny the gathering need for him, the growing tension that seemed to suddenly fill her.

Was need enough? Was wanting enough? She opened her eyes and froze at the reflection she saw in the mirror. She had dressed in white. Virginal white.

Bride white—for a woman who isn't a bride?

But . . . I . . . love him . . . .

The feeling of panic left. Sarah drew a deep breath. She was in love with Lucas Rockworth. Why had it taken her until now to realize that?

It was her love for him that was urging her to bond with him in the primary way nature had decreed a man and woman should bond. There was so much more than passion between them. And yet the passion could not be ignored or denied.

Celibacy?

Sarah laughed at her childish schemes for short-circuiting what life was supposed to be all about—growing up and accepting everything that the growing up entailed.

She would go to him. And tell him of her love. And maybe it would happen tonight—that special bonding. But it would happen only if Lucas could tell her that he loved her, too. She was worth that, worth a declaration of love. She'd settle for nothing less.

"Sarah!" With the shout of her name came a simultaneous pounding on the bathroom door.

Sarah opened the door and encountered Deborah's animated features. "What's—"

"Ryan just drove up."

"What's he doing *here*?"

"Who knows? But I can guarantee he didn't come to see me."

"Let him in while I put on my shoes."

Deborah took the white sneakers from Sarah. "Uh-uh, you answer the door. You can put your shoes on later."

"Honestly, Deborah, I know you and Ryan don't get along, but is it asking too much for you to—"

"Yes!"

Ryan's loud knock discouraged further conversation. Sarah padded to the door, knowing Deborah wouldn't poke her head inside the motor home's tiny living room until her brother had left.

"Ryan, hello!" Sarah told herself it was foolish to be intimidated by her brother. And yet, for as long as she could remember, the ten years separating them had been a formidable barrier.

"Hello, Sarah." He stepped inside the motor home.

She studied his grim features and then sighed. Instead of a romantic interlude with Lucas, it looked as if she was going to have some kind of confrontation with her brother.

"What brings you to Grey Horse Lake?" she asked brightly.

He glanced around the compact living area. "Where is everyone?"

"Wendy went to the movies with Julie, Lucas's niece."

His features relaxed. "Deborah drove them into Sandpoint?"

"No, Lucas's housekeeper took them." Sarah thought of Lucas and their moonlit encounter. She didn't want to be late. "Surely you didn't drive all this way to find out what everyone was doing?"

"Why didn't Deborah go with them? Where is she?"

Sarah groaned in exasperation. At this rate, she and her brother would be locked in a marathon discussion. She needed to speed things up.

"Deborah is in the back bedroom." *Holding my shoes hostage.* "Why are you here?"

"Is she sick?"

"No. Why are you here?"

Ryan smiled ruefully, and Sarah stared at him in surprise. She'd forgotten how drop-dead handsome her older brother was. "Maybe I got homesick."

"You don't live here. By the way, thank you for loaning us the motor home."

"You're welcome." Ryan's dark eyes sparkled with amusement. "Aren't you going to invite me to sit down?"

Sarah gestured to a bench seat and claimed the one opposite it. "Comfy?" she inquired sweetly, after he'd scrunched his long body around the table separating them.

"Going to offer me some coffee?" he suggested hopefully.

Sarah frowned at him. "All we've got is instant. You *hate* instant."

"Yeah, I do at that." He rested his elbows on the table and steepled his fingertips. "I guess you're wondering what I'm doing here...."

Sarah rolled her eyes. Even under the best of circumstances, she wasn't a patient person. "The thought did cross my mind."

"Mom and Dad were going over the monthly report the other day. It's the first time in four years your name wasn't on it. We got to talking about you, wondering how things were coming along up here. I was nominated to find out."

"You volunteered," Sarah accused.

Ryan smiled. "I guess maybe I did. Sorry, pudden, I just couldn't help myself."

At the mention of her childhood name, Sarah's mouth curved. "Ryan, when I was two years old, you could get away with calling me 'pudden.'"

"Some habits are hard to break."

"Well, things are going great," Sarah said firmly, hoping to hurry her brother on his way.

"I noticed the marked-off areas. Looks like you've been busy. Who's going to do the building, a local company?"

Ryan's voice had harshened, and Sarah had a feeling they were on a collision course with the subject of Lucas Rockworth.

"This was our original plan," she hedged.

His eyes narrowed. "And now?"

Sighing, Sarah decided there was no point in putting off the inevitable. "And now Rockworth Construction is going to erect Camp Grey Horse."

"Small world, isn't it?" Ryan asked softly.

"Sometimes."

"How did you and Rockworth hook up, Sarah?"

This wasn't the first time she'd thought her brother would have made an excellent attorney. He had the instincts of a lethal cross-examiner.

"We ran into each other my first morning at the lake. I told you that over the telephone."

"I remember. Sounds as if one thing led to another. You meet the guy. Live with him for a week. And then pay him a small fortune—for the privilege of building your camp."

"Now just a minute, I didn't "live" with Lucas— not the way you're implying. It just so happens that he's a very generous man, and he had some extra room at his cabin. He graciously took me in."

This time it was Ryan who rolled his eyes. "Come on, Sarah. If Lucas Rockworth offered you a place to stay, it's because he's attracted to you. He took advantage of you being stranded, so he could get close to you—*some* generosity."

Sarah's eyes flashed. "You're wrong, Ryan. Lucas Rockworth isn't that kind of man. He wouldn't know *how* to take advantage of someone. He's gentle and sweet and . . . a bit shy."

Ryan snickered. "Good Lord, Sarah, listen to yourself. You're describing St. Francis of Assisi. I've been in the trenches with Rockworth. In business, he's a tough street fighter. Don't tell me he conducts his personal life any differently."

"You're being ridiculous. Lucas isn't a . . . a shark. When you and he were 'in the trenches' as you put it, you annihilated him. He didn't stand a chance against your bullying tactics."

Ryan laughed outright. "Sarah, wake up. Lucas didn't lose a dime in our deal. The penalty check he received because Deborah backed out of selling her property more than compensated him for his time. Believe me, Rockworth is one shrewd operator. He knows all the angles, and he plays them—like a pro."

Sarah shook her head. "I don't know how Lucas handles his business affairs, but I do know he's a very gentle person. I'm in love with him, Ryan."

"Damn."

"Well, thanks a lot. I tell you I'm in love, and you swear at me."

"I'm not swearing at you, pudden. It's just that your track record with men isn't all that great. Just a couple of months ago you were in love with Ned Ranklin, remember?"

Sarah did remember. She flushed. "This is different. Lucas is nothing like Ned. Even more important, *I'm* different. Besides, I wasn't really in love with Ned. I was just flattered by his sudden attention. I let his sophistication and suave manners sweep me off my feet. Believe me, this time my feet are planted on solid earth." She curled her toes.

"I'd believe you, if you didn't have stars in your eyes. Sarah, the man you've described to me simply isn't Lucas Rockworth. Stay involved with him, and he's going to break your heart."

"You just don't believe in love. Look at you. You're thirty-six and you've never married."

"That's because when I marry, it's going to be for forever. And I haven't met the woman I want to spend forever with—yet."

"Well, I've met the man I want."

"Are you talking marriage?" His voice hardened.

Sarah raised her chin. "We're getting to know each other a little...better and working our way up to marriage."

Ryan jumped to his feet. "I'll kill him."

"Oh, no, you won't! You leave Lucas alone." Sarah also stood.

"I'll leave him alone, all right. After I find out what his intentions are." Ryan moved to the door.

"Stop! You can't go barging in on Lucas, demanding what his intentions are toward me."

Ryan opened the door and glared at her over his shoulder. "Why the hell not?"

"Because—because I haven't seduced him yet, and you'll scare him away."

"Oh, Lord, give me patience."

Sarah stared after her departing brother and wailed. Deborah came rushing out of the bedroom.

"Sarah, what's wrong? What happened?"

"I've got to stop Ryan. He's going to ruin everything."

"You're not going anywhere without your shoes," Deborah protested.

Sarah stared down at her bare feet. "Oh, spit."

"Relax, it'll only take you a minute to put them on. You can use the time to tell me what's happening."

"Ryan is going to Lucas's cabin." Sarah struggled with her knotted laces.

"Uh-oh."

"Exactly."

"What does Ryan hope to accomplish?"

"I'm not sure. He either wants to kill Lucas or force him to marry me. I think." Sarah got her last shoe tied and stood.

Both she and Deborah reached the door at the same time. "Where are you going?"

"With you. There's no way I'm going to let you go charging into a lions' den with two snarling lions."

Sarah touched Deborah's arm. "There's just one lion—my brother. Lucas is a lamb."

"I've been meaning to talk to you about that, Sarah. Whatever gave you the idea that Lucas Rockworth is some kind of wimp?"

"He's not a wimp! He's just...shy and...sensitive."

"Lucas Rockworth?"

"Yes, and it'll embarrass him for you to see Ryan chew him up and spit him out."

"Lucas Rock—"

"Wait here—please?"

"Okay, but if you're not back in twenty minutes, I'm coming after you."

When Sarah reached Lucas's porch she heard her brother's angry voice ricocheting off the cabin's walls. She pushed open the front door. Ryan's voice was coming from the back sun deck. Loudly. Air traffic at twenty-thousand feet could probably hear his tirade against Lucas. She moved quickly toward the deck.

"I don't know what kind of game you're playing with my sister, but if I find out you've laid a hand on her, I'm going to take you apart—piece by piece."

"Then you might as well get started. I've laid both hands on her, and I intend to keep on doing it."

The rock-hard fury of Lucas's voice struck Sarah like the blast of a furnace. She stood at the partially opened door, stunned as she watched the taut confrontation.

Ryan raised his brows. "I don't get it. How did you convince Sarah you're some kind of knight in shining armor?"

Lucas flushed. "You're exaggerating."

"The hell I am. When Sarah describes you, it sounds like she's tallying up a list of requirements for sainthood."

"That's between me and Sarah."

"No, it's not. Because I won't stand by and watch you hurt her. Sarah's one of the special ones. She believes, she trusts, she...dreams. I won't let you destroy her dreams."

"And you think I would?"

"You're as hard as set concrete, Rockworth. And Sarah's as soft as rose petals."

"Sarah's tougher than you think."

"Hurt her and I'll ruin you."

Lucas laughed harshly, and Sarah shuddered.

"Rockworth Construction could swallow Burke Realty in one bite."

Deborah had been right! Ryan and Lucas were both...lions—and from the sound of it, about to rip each other apart.

"I'd see you dead before I'd stand by and watch you break Sarah's heart." Ryan's voice was devoid of passion, yet deadly in its softness.

"Your threat is worthless, Burke."

"You don't think I mean it?"

"You mean it."

"And?"

"And I protect what's mine, Burke. I consider Sarah mine."

There was a thick pause before her brother acknowledged Lucas's challenge. "And I suppose Sarah considers herself...*yours*?"

"Before the night's over, I'll make sure of it."

"That's a helluva thing to tell a man about his sister."

"When a brother butts into his sister's business, he runs the risk of hearing some hard truths."

"Bottom line—hurt her and you'll pay."

"Bottom line—Sarah is mine, and I'll take care of her."

Ryan laughed harshly. "Think you can fit into the family?"

"Count on it."

"Since we understand each other then, let's settle this with a handshake."

Sarah watched her brother extend his hand. Lucas accepted it.

"Do we consider this a binding contract?"

Her brother laughed again. "You're one tough bastard, Rockworth."

"Wait until you meet my father."

Sarah backed slowly away from the doorway. If she hadn't heard Lucas with her own ears, she would not have believed him capable of such brutal toughness. She *had* heard him, and she still couldn't come to terms with the fact that her tender, gentle lover-to-be was... Why he was Rambo, after all!

She turned from the cabin and followed the path back to the motor home. Over and over she replayed the fierce confrontation she'd heard. It didn't make sense. How could she have thought Lucas was a gentle, caring man—a man incapable of the bullying tactics she'd come to associate with her brother?

Sarah could feel the burning pressure of tears fill her eyes. She'd only just realized she was in love. She brushed at the falling tears with the back of her hand and looked around. Dusk had come. Dusk had come, and she'd discovered the man she was in love with didn't exist.

Sweet, gentle Lucas Rockworth simply was not. She had given her heart and planned on giving her body to a phantom, a creature of her own imagination.

Creature was an excellent word, she thought, her tears drying. There was no way she could have been so mistaken about Lucas Rockworth without him deliberately misleading her. She remembered one of their first conversations. He'd asked her straight out. Who appealed to her more? Rambo or Mr. Rogers?

She's picked Mr. Rogers and voilá! He had appeared. Shy. Sweet. Sensitive. The dirty rat! He'd done it on purpose, played the role of a modern, tender man. Good grief, if she'd picked Rambo, he probably would have greased up his body, looped ammo belts around his neck and stuck a butcher knife between his teeth.

She'd had him reading poetry!

"Sarah, where are you going? What happened?"

Deborah's worried voice penetrated Sarah's dazed thoughts. She'd almost passed her friend on the path to the motor home.

Sarah turned around. "You were right."

"About what? Sarah, what's wrong? You look like you're in shock."

"I probably am."

"My Lord, did they actually get into a brawl? *What* happened?"

"There was no fight. You were right. Lucas was perfectly capable of handling Ryan."

"But—"

"Don't worry about it. Ryan's fine. Lucas is fine. Actually I think they have the makings of a solid friendship."

"*What?*"

"They have so much in common, you know—*my* welfare."

"That doesn't surprise me," Deborah said.

"And then there's the fact that they're on the same wavelength. When you get right down to it, you could almost call them blood brothers. They both look at the world in the same determined way." Sarah moved away.

"Where are you going?"

"To change my clothes."

Chapter Nine

Sarah's gait was determined as she strode up the path to Lucas's cabin. It was another glorious morning at Grey Horse Lake. The sun, lake and forest were in serene accord. Fresh mountain air, replete with the scents of pine, meadow grass and wildflowers, hung richly about her.

The tan purse she carried under her arm felt strange. During the past few weeks, she'd forgotten what it felt like to carry the once familiar burden. And yet until recently, both her purse and leather briefcase had been constant companions.

Her thoughts drifted to her conversation with Ryan when he'd returned to the motor home. Her brother had talked about her role at Burke Realty. She had been astonished to learn that as the firm's newest member, she'd been making a valuable contribution. The clients she'd dealt with were requesting her to handle their future transactions.

Ryan had showed her his sales printouts from when he'd first begun with the firm, comparing them against hers. Incredible as it was, she had actually outperformed her dynamic brother. He'd gone on to express their parents' wish that she spend only her summers managing Camp Grey Horse. But each fall, they hoped she would return to Spokane, to the family business.

Lucas's cabin came into view. *He* was the one subject she and her brother hadn't discussed. Sarah shook her head in frustration. It seemed that once again she was the victim of a broken heart.

Her lips thinned. She refused to think of herself as a victim. Lucas Rockworth was the victim—of his own devious making. Simmering anger throbbed at Sarah's temples, obliterating the question of *why* Lucas had pretended to be something he was not.

After marching up its steps, Sarah knocked briskly at the cabin's door. While she waited for someone to answer, she squared her shoulders and adopted a cheerful smile.

When the door swung open, Sarah found herself looking into Lucas's handsome face. She forced her smile to remain intact.

"Good morning, Lucas. I dropped by to see if I could ask a favor."

Lucas regarded Sarah's nonchalant pose for several seconds before stepping onto the porch and closing the door behind him.

"I waited for you."

Sarah feigned a look of confusion. "Waited for me? When?"

"Last night—at the lake."

I'll just bet you did! "Oh. It was so late after Ryan left that I decided to call it a night."

Lucas stared at her intently, his dark eyes probing the contours of her face. "So he stayed late?"

"Um-hmm." Sarah hung on to her vacuous smile.

"Did he . . . did he say something to you about me? Something that changed your mind about keeping our rendezvous?"

She swallowed and felt tears begin to build. Blinking furiously, she forced herself to subdue them. Hadn't she cried enough over this . . . this scurrilous impostor?

"It wasn't anything Ryan said that discouraged me from coming." She forced herself to lean closer to him and smile conspiratorially. Lucas Rockworth wasn't the only one who could act. "Actually I was thinking of you."

"Thinking what?"

"Well, both of us know what a shy man you are, right?"

He nodded slowly.

"A real sweetheart of a fellow," Sarah mumbled under her breath.

"What?"

"I said you're a real gentle fellow. Ryan told me that you and he practically had a knock-down-drag-out fight, and I figured that you were probably pretty shaken by the confrontation."

"Not really," Lucas returned coolly. Sarah's dramatic posturing had begun to grate on his nerves.

"Oh, well, of course, *now* you can say that. But I bet last night you were a quivering mass of insecurity. I suppose I could have brought you some hot cocoa to calm your nerves. . . . But somehow that idea didn't appeal to me—not when I'd been looking forward to a night of raw passion and . . . and wild sex."

"Sarah!"

"Don't look so shocked, Lucas. A woman has . . . needs. Of course a man like you probably isn't comfortable with a real woman, but I was going to allow for your . . . timidness and be really gentle with you." Her smile had shrunk to a baring of white teeth.

A muscle jumped in Lucas's cheek. "Sarah, this has gone far enough."

"Perhaps you're right. We'd best save this conversation for another time—when you're calmer."

Lucas's dark eyes glittered with a primitive savagery that made Sarah wonder how she could have so badly misjudged his disposition. Beastly man. Beastly tempered. And probably a beastly lover. She should have recognized his true nature when they first met. He was a carbon copy of the tyrannical brother she'd grown up with.

Lucas Rockworth continued to stare at Sarah Burke as if she were a bizarre life-form.

"Got your pickup keys on you?"

At Sarah's irrelevant question, his gaze narrowed. "Why?"

"I need to run into Sandpoint. As you know, Deborah's and my only form of transportation is the motor home. Since you've lent us your Jeep before, I figured you wouldn't mind letting me borrow it this morning."

Lucas reached into his pocket, never taking his eyes from Sarah. Her brother had done something, said something that had turned her against him. So much for the honor of a handshake.

He extended the keys of his new Jeep Cherokee. He'd bought the pickup only a month earlier, specifically for his sojourn at the lake.

The golden keys he dangled in front of Sarah caught and reflected the dancing rays of the morning sun. Several seconds skittered by before he dropped them into her outstretched palm.

"I don't suppose in your present mood you'd like some company?"

Sarah squirmed under Lucas's level stare. It simply wasn't part of her nature to be rude or devious. Despite what she knew of him, Lucas's quiet regard made her feel guilty at her shrewish behavior. She could feel herself softening toward him. She swallowed again. It seemed a woman's dreams died hard.

Standing in the sunlight of a new morning, Sarah could almost believe Lucas had been sincere with her—that he was a gentle, caring man. He was so vital, so strong, so manly. She felt herself being pulled toward him, toward the pain-pleasure she knew he could give her.

Was this how an animal felt when trapped in a hunter's snare? Helpless? And when the hunter finally came to tend his trap, did numbing chemicals deliver a gentle mercy to his victim?

Held by Lucas's dark eyes, Sarah was shocked by the knowledge that she still wanted him. Still wanted to feel his hands, his mouth, his body crowding close against her. Still wanted the gentle mercy his possession would deliver.

Then Lucas made the mistake of smiling. Cautious concern seemed to fill his eyes, breaking the mindless spell in which he'd trapped her.

"What's wrong, Sarah?"

You are! For me . . . Sarah gripped his keys tightly in her hand. She wasn't about to fall for a second verse of his "sensitive man" routine.

"Headache," she explained, stepping back. "I'll be back in a couple of hours with your truck."

"Sarah—"

"*Ciao*, Lucas."

Lucas watched Sarah hurry down the front steps. He could have easily caught up with her and forced his company for the ride to Sandpoint. He rubbed his hand across the back of his neck. Somehow he didn't think Sarah would appreciate being strong-armed today.

Hell, she probably didn't think he was capable of strong-arming a gnat. She had him pegged as an emotional ninety-pound weakling. Well, all that was going to change.

He was going to make love to Miss Sarah Burke. And when he did, she would discover she had a tiger by the tail. He watched her back his Jeep from its cement pad and smoothly angle it out onto the gravel road leading to town. Small explosions of dust followed her departure.

Yeah. It would be no more Mr. Nice Guy. Sarah was about to meet the real Lucas Rockworth.

Several exhausting but satisfying hours later, Sarah entered the motor home. Deborah stood at the gas range, stirring the contents of a medium-size pot. Sarah noticed the small table was set for two.

"Isn't Wendy eating with us?"

Deborah shook her head. "There's no way I can compete with Tansy's cooking *and* Julie Quincy's company."

Sarah dropped her purse onto a padded bench seat. "It doesn't bother you, does it—Wendy spending so much time with Julie?"

Deborah frowned. "I'm being adult about the situation. Wendy's budding friendship with Lucas's niece is providing me with lots of uninterrupted time to catch up with our correspondence. It's just that I... Oh, I'm being foolish."

Sarah studied her friend's shadowed features. "About what?"

Deborah laid the spoon aside and placed a lid on the pan. She took a moment to adjust the blue flame beneath it, then turned to Sarah.

"I...I've always had this feeling about Wendy. As...as if our time together wasn't going to be long." A haunted expression touched Deborah's eyes. "Wh-when she was in the car accident and she survived, the feeling faded. It was as if I'd passed some terrible crisis with Wendy, and she'd been spared."

Sarah said nothing, deciding that it was important for her friend to share her feelings. Deborah moved to the table and claimed the bench seat across from her.

"I was looking forward to us being together at the lake. We'd spend time with each other. Get close again. It's been over a year since the wreck, Sarah. And she hasn't once spoken to me about it—about how she feels being trapped in that damned wheelchair. I wanted this time—I *needed* this time with her."

"And she's turned to Julie Quincy?" Sarah observed softly.

"And I'm being unreasonable and jealous." Deborah's eyes filled with pain. "But the feeling has come back, Sarah. The feeling that I'm going to...to *lose* Wendy. I'm afraid every moment we're apart. I can barely concentrate on the applications I'm reviewing from our prospective camp counselors, and I'm not doing much more than writing form letters to the parents of the children we've enrolled for the July session. I'm failing you as your business partner. And... and I'm becoming hopelessly neurotic where my daughter's concerned.''

Sarah reached across the table and pulled her friend's icy hands into hers. "Honey, it's not neurotic for you to feel overprotective toward Wendy. She almost *died*. Of course, you're going to be preoccupied with losing her. The wreck reminded you of your own mortality, and it damned near proved Wendy's.''

Tears shimmered in Deborah's gray eyes. "But I'm failing the two most important people in my life!''

Uncomfortably Sarah recalled the past few weeks. She'd let Lucas totally absorb her thoughts, shifting Camp Grey Horse to second place in her priorities. "I think I'm the one who should be apologizing. I let my infatuation with a... a sneaky manipulator sidetrack me.''

The haunted expression in Deborah's eyes faded. "What has Lucas done to make you angry?''

"Shown his true colors. And they were as black as his reprehensible heart!''

"I knew you had something on your mind after you came back from his cabin last night, but all I could get out of you were dire mutterings about men in general.''

"There's got to have been a good man—once,'' Sarah said bleakly.

"What makes you think so?''

"I'm not sure.... Do you suppose Santa Claus was the last good man?''

"I always had the feeling it was Mrs. Claus who did the legwork for him—you know, deciding that little Maria should get the doll and Dimitri, the sled."

"You're probably right. I bet *Mrs.* Rogers writes all of Mr. Rogers's material. He probably hates kids."

"Do you suppose Albert Schweitzer stepped on ants when nobody was looking?"

Sarah looked into Deborah's teasing eyes and laughed. "Now you've gone too far. I've got to believe in Albert."

"Well, then, there you go. He was the last good man."

"I don't know, Deborah. Maybe we're being too hard on them. Ryan did lend us this beautiful motor home."

"Lucas lent you his Jeep today."

A feral gleam flickered in Sarah's normally good-natured gaze. "And I returned it to him. I consider us even."

"Until you want to borrow it again?"

"I rented a car for us in Sandpoint. Odell Brewster is driving it out for us."

"Who's Odell Brewster?"

The gleam lapped over into Sarah's smile. "The general contractor I hired today to build Camp Grey Horse."

"What!"

"His was the next lowest bid after Lucas's."

"But I thought—"

"I refuse to use a firm whose president is a dyed-in-the-wool snake in the grass."

"Oh, Sarah, honey, even *I* have faith in Lucas's professional integrity. I wish you had consulted me. When you cool down you're going to—"

"I know I should have discussed this with you, but I didn't want to be talked out of anything. Mr. Brewster is every bit as qualified as Lucas. And I'm not *going* to cool down. I—I refuse to cool down. I'm going to stay good and mad at that—that *man* for a long, long time."

Lucas stared in dissatisfaction at his Jeep Cherokee. Sarah had returned it in mint condition three days earlier, and he hadn't spoken with her since. She'd been impossible to catch up with. The few times he had caught glimpses of her she'd been behind the steering wheel of the saucy red van she must have leased in Sandpoint.

Lucas squinted against the sun's reflection that bounced off his Jeep's glossy exterior. The harsh glare seemed to highlight a nick on the driver's door. He closed the distance between himself and the Jeep, running his fingertips over the blue paint. Instead of a nick, he dislodged a flattened bug.

For no good reason, he gave the pickup's front tire a hearty kick. Through his canvas shoe, pain shot from his toes to his eyebrows. He forced himself to summon enough dignity to refrain from massaging his foot.

"Feel better?" Julie's voice drifted cheerfully from his cabin's front porch.

Lucas looked over to where she stood. His niece's blue eyes seemed filled with a feminine superiority far beyond her years. He scowled at her, offended at how easily she'd apparently gotten over her crush on him. Women were fickle. Lucas realized he was hardly the first man to reach that conclusion.

"They're making tires harder than they used to."

Julie straightened from her slouched position. "You mean back in the good old days?"

Lucas's scowl darkened. It occurred to him that since Sarah had blazed into his life, he no longer got the respect he used to command. "Yeah, back in the good old days." Experimentally he wiggled his injured toes. They and his entire foot throbbed.

"Why don't you go see her?"

"I will."

"When?"

"When she's had time to cool down and realize her big, bad brother fed her a lot of bull about me."

Lucas hated admitting how much it bothered him that Sarah had turned against him without giving him an opportunity to defend himself against her brother's...truths? If the tables were turned he would have given Sarah the chance to tell her side of the story.

Hell, he would have given her a hundred chances. And she couldn't give him a lousy five minutes to plead his case. He had thought he meant more to Sarah than a quick brush-off. He had thought...

He had thought maybe she was falling in love with him.

Lucas stared pensively at the path that led from his cabin to where he knew he would find Sarah. He'd given her three days to cool down. He drew himself to his full height. Three days were long enough. Unconsciously he took one step, then another along the path, toward Camp Grey Horse.

"See you later, Uncle Lucas."

Lucas didn't hear his niece's farewell. His gaze, his thoughts were already a quarter of a mile away.

"What do you think, Mr. Brewster? Can you meet a June thirtieth deadline?" Sarah shaded her eyes and stared into Odell Brewster's weather-beaten face.

The general contractor's measuring gaze raked the dilapidated motel units and then dropped to the blue-prints his large, work-roughened hands were in the process of rolling up. He shifted his massive frame to his left side and spat.

Sarah tried not to cringe. Judiciously she took a casual step to her left—away from...from whatever Mr. Odell Brewster no longer wished to have residing inside his mouth.

"Be easier—cheaper—to tear down what's here and start over. Quicker, too."

Sarah took another step to her left. Mr. Brewster's mouth seemed to be at work, apparently about to rid itself of another...unwelcome something.

"I realize that, but restoring the bungalows has a special appeal to Ms. Scott and myself."

"Well, then, that's that." He spat and then smiled widely.

Sarah reminded herself that good dental hygiene or the lack thereof in no way reflected a man's ability as a contractor. "When do you think you can get started?"

Mr. Brewster looked at the sun instead of his watch. "Tomorrow. Early. Big job over in Sandpoint got canceled. Financing fell through. Carpenters, electricians, plumbers—all scrambling to fill the hole in their summer workload."

"Oh."

He pulled the plastic bill of his blue cap over his perspiring, multilined forehead. Shocks of white hair rearranged themselves. "You're lucky you called me.

I work fast and good. I won't shortchange you, either.''

"I appreciate you coming out so promptly."

"No problem." He moved toward his battered pickup.

Sarah followed him to the ancient vehicle. It looked as if it had been driven through a hip-high mud hole, dive-bombed by a squadron of bugs and then sprinkled liberally with cement dust. Where there wasn't rust, there were major dents.

She reminded herself that one couldn't judge a man's worth by what he drove. Lucas Rockworth drove a shiny new Cherokee.

Mr. Brewster paused beside his truck, spat, applied his big fingers to its stubborn door handle, grunted and then climbed inside. "See you in the morning. Early."

"Early," Sarah confirmed, jumping back when the truck bucked to life.

She watched the pickup demolish the mountain grass and wildflowers that bordered the gravel road leading to the main highway into town.

So the man looked like a derelict, drove like a lunatic and spat like a major-league baseball player. He had a sound reputation in the building trade. That's what counted. Not his manners.

After committing the folly of falling in love with Lucas Rockworth, a man with excellent manners, she would never again quibble over someone else's social graces.

The dust Mr. Brewster's truck had kicked up drifted slowly back to earth. At least the contractor hadn't scratched himself in any embarrassing places.

"Who was that?"

Sarah spun around at Lucas's friendly question.

Chapter Ten

How dare he?

How dare he show his handsome, conniving face in her presence? She sneaked a glance at his snug-fitting, faded jeans.

And how dare he flaunt his muscular body on her...premises? Sparks of outrage shimmered in her brown eyes, and her pupils narrowed to pinpoint diameter.

Sarah's fierce expression caught Lucas off guard. He retreated a step, unprepared for the surge of excitement that shot through him when he confronted her anger.

Staring into her flushed face, Lucas wondered if any man, who felt the fire simmering beneath his skin as he felt it, would forego the thrill of the chase, capture and surrender. Lucas smiled grimly, acknowledging that the surrender would be his. His body, his heart and all his earthly possessions.

He reclaimed the path of territory he'd yielded.

"Odell Brewster." Sarah's chin tilted pugnaciously.

Lucas blinked. One moment he was charging down a hill to sweep his woman into his arms, and the next he was desperately trying to keep one step ahead of her. Would she always run pell-mell through life?

"What?"

"Odell Brewster! The man who just left. You asked me who he was," Sarah explained, exasperated at how difficult it was to remain furious with Lucas. Somehow when that slightly out-of-focus look drifted into his eyes, her heart always took a peculiar lurch.

"Was he looking for directions?" Since the other summer cabins had become occupied, traffic around the lake had increased dramatically.

"Odell Brewster is the general contractor I hired in Sandpoint. He's going to be in charge of building Camp Grey Horse." Sarah waited for the flush of victory she'd expected to feel when she made her grand announcement. But as she stared into Lucas's stunned, then angry features, the flush fizzled.

"I thought Rockworth Construction was going to do the work," he pointed out with menacing softness.

"I decided to use someone else."

"Why?"

"Because I refuse to work with a dishonest, disreputable... phony!" She could feel tears building behind her eyes—tears she'd die before shedding in Lucas's presence.

Lucas's hands gripped her shoulders without gentleness. "What did your brother tell you about me,

Sarah? Don't you think you owe me the courtesy of allowing me to defend myself?''

"Defend yourself! You already did that...admirably."

He increased the pressure of his grip and gave her a little shake. "Damn you, Sarah, I'm not in the mood for guessing games. What happened to change you from a warm—" He broke off and pulled her against him. "No, change that. What changed you from a *hot* lover to—"

She pushed against his chest, trying futilely to free herself. "Would-be, almost lover—there's a big difference, Lucas."

"Only in minutes, honey. Only in minutes." His mouth came down on hers. Hard, hungry and *hot*.

To Sarah's horror, she felt herself begin to respond to his urgent lovemaking. In frustration she stamped her foot. It connected with Lucas's.

"*Damn!*" Lucas's heartfelt exclamation terminated his angry kiss. But he didn't let her go. "This romance business has its drawbacks."

At the husky observation, a teasing look crept into his gaze. Sarah stared up at him in momentary confusion. Then the meaning of his words registered, and she commenced a valiant effort to squirm free from his embrace. She succeeded.

"*Romance!* You wouldn't recognize something romantic if it fell on top of you." She shook her hair free from her eyes and placed both hands on her hips.

Lucas felt a flash fire of hunger race through him. He closed his hands into fists and jammed them into his pockets. Sarah looked mad enough to make good on the threat her brother had delivered several nights ago.

"When you fell from the sky, I caught you. I consider that very romantic." He smiled crookedly.

Sarah felt her heart go bump. She ignored the strangely pleasant sensation. "Don't try your Mr. Nice Guy routine on me, Lucas Rockworth. I know you're nothing but a . . . a wolf in sheep's clothing!"

"Your brother must have told all manner of evil against me."

"*You* told me. With your own sneaky lips. I went to your cabin to defend you. But guess what? You're as big a bully as Ryan!"

"So you went tearing off to my cabin to protect me from your big, bad brother, hmmm?"

Sarah didn't like the speculative look Lucas subjected her to. "I didn't want Ryan to crush your gentle spirit."

"And when you got to the cabin, you found out that I could take care of myself—right?"

"Against him and the entire division of marines," Sarah said glumly.

"And you didn't like that, did you? You wanted to be the one to make your brother back down."

"I *wanted* to help you, protect you against—"

"You should have joined us then. I wouldn't have turned down your help."

"But you didn't need me! You don't need me. You're as strong and as tough as the steel your Jeep's made from."

Lucas felt the throbbing in his injured foot and wondered if he should take off his shoe and sock. Perhaps if he showed Sarah he was imminently hurtable, she would come back into his arms.

"Honey, no man is as big a wimp as you had yourself talked into believing I was."

"You weren't a wimp!"

"No, I was just so darn sensitive and tenderhearted I could wear a Santa suit three hundred and sixty five days of the year."

Sarah conveniently forgot her own recent comments on the jolly old fellow. "Only a *cad* would say something derogatory about Santa Claus."

"You got him lined up to be your next boyfriend? I got news for you, honey. He's married. And so's Mr. Rogers."

"Notice there's no *Mrs.* Rambo."

"Yet."

"Ever!"

"Ah, Sarah, so I'm not quite the wimp you thought I was? There's a whole other side of me you might like—if you gave yourself permission to spend time with a real man."

Sarah found herself sputtering. "*You're* nothing like the man I fell in—" In horror, she bit off her announcement.

Lucas raised his brows. "How do you know?"

"I know, Lucas Rockworth. I know you're a brute and a bully. And . . . and . . ."

"And?"

"Oh, go jump in a lake."

"Come with me. We'll go skinny-dipping."

"Go without me."

He tipped back his head and laughed. "What I have in mind is no fun by yourself."

Sarah debated tromping on his other foot. Insensitive clod!

A wicked grin slashed Lucas's handsome features. "And I know who I want for company. She's about five-foot-five, has flashing brown eyes and a sharp, but tasty little tongue.''

"You just forget about my tongue. And every other part of me. As of this moment you can consider me off-limits.''

"No way, honey. The way I see it, now I'm free to pursue you the way a man goes after a woman he wants. No holds barred. With everything I've got.''

Sarah allowed herself a teeny peek at his virile body. Everything he had...was plenty! "Well, the way *I* see it, you're on private property, Mr. Rockworth. In short, you're a trespasser.''

He raised his hand and ran the roughened tip of his forefinger down her cheek. Sarah stood perfectly still, firmly ordering her nerve endings to simmer down, not up.

"You don't really want to use another contractor to build Camp Grey Horse.''

Sarah refused to comment. Instead, she repeated the alphabet to herself backward. She'd gotten to *M* when Lucas's callused palm caressed her cheek. Against his tenderness, she discovered the alphabet proved a puny distraction.

She felt her gaze pulled irresistibly to his. And with one simple look, he embraced her more passionately than any man who'd urged her to make love. She stared into his dark eyes, confused and more than a little afraid. Why didn't it matter that she knew the truth of what kind of man he was? Why hadn't the special power he seemed to have over her lost its magic?

His palm moved gently against her cheek, then dropped slowly to her throat. She felt the muscles around her mouth relax and her lips part. It shocked her that . . . that she still wanted him—intimately, completely. She tried to shake her head against that knowledge, but his touch held her captive. His touch and his gaze.

Sarah licked her lips. "I've already signed a contract."

Lucas's face went cold, and he dropped his hand. "You knew how much I was looking forward to my construction company building your camp."

She nodded. But when she'd called Brewster, she'd told herself that Lucas Rockworth was a phony, incapable of sincerity. That his offer to build Camp Grey Horse hadn't meant anything special to him.

Now as she stared into his furious features, it occurred to her that even though Lucas wasn't the saint she'd imagined, he was no villain, either. And all at once she regretted her impetuous trip to Sandpoint. She should have had this discussion with Lucas first, should have found out exactly who Lucas Rockworth was.

"Then I guess we don't have anything to talk about. Goodbye, Sarah."

He turned and walked away. After a few twisting turns of the path, he disappeared behind the pines.

Tears stung Sarah's eyes. It seemed Deborah had been right, after all. She did regret trying to pay Lucas back for his deception. Regretted it bitterly.

The lake was as black as the clouded sky that stretched above it. Sarah stopped long enough to zip her windbreaker. A breeze had come up, chilling the night air. One week had passed since she and Lucas had quarreled.

She began walking again, across the packed sand that cradled the restless lake. Only as she looked back on their argument did she realize that at first Lucas hadn't been all that angry. Initially their confrontation had been almost playful.

It had been when Lucas had realized she'd signed a contract with Brewster that his manner had turned cold. Sarah sighed. Since their quarrel, she'd learned that one did not negate a signed contract with Odell Brewster. Unless one wanted to pay an exorbitant penalty fee. At this point, neither she nor Deborah was willing to throw away Camp Grey Horse's operating capital.

She missed Lucas terribly.

She was still furious with him, of course. But in the past few days she'd become aware of feelings other than anger. She was hurt that during the time she'd been falling in love with him, he'd been playing a charade with her.

Her heart was broken.

How many times would this happen to her? Her former fiancé's face crept into her thoughts. But his image was blurred.

Again Sarah stopped walking. She drew her arms around her, knowing instinctively that months, even years, from now when she tried to remember Lucas, his image would be crystal clear.

No, what was she thinking of? She wouldn't be trying to remember Lucas. She'd be trying to forget him, to strip him clean from her memory. But she knew she would not be successful. Tears came to her eyes. She didn't want to forget him, anyway. Not really.

When Sarah recalled her confrontation with Lucas, a poignant smile curved her lips. Lucas Rockworth... She hated to admit it, but when he'd announced that he was free to pursue her the way a man pursued a woman—with no holds barred—she'd found his cockiness rather endearing....

She stiffened. Where had that thought come from? He hadn't been endearing. Besides, male arrogance was something she'd had to tolerate from Ryan all her life. And she'd concluded years ago that a cocky, dominating and *arrogant* man would never have a place in her life.

Still, she hadn't meant to hurt him. And in those last few seconds with Lucas, when she'd told him that she had signed a contract with Brewster, she'd understood that her actions had hurt him.

And now he was furious with her.

Which should have made them even. But somehow, it didn't.

Slowly Sarah's whereabouts penetrated her confused thoughts. The lights from Lucas's cabin lit the area around her. She supposed she could lie to herself and say that she hadn't meant to go to him. But what would that accomplish? They needed to talk.

She was an adult, not a child. Outbursts of anger might provide momentary release, but she refused to live her life on a roller coaster of emotion. She supposed it was that maturity that made her feelings different from those Julie had felt toward Lucas. A schoolgirl could afford the luxury of a crush. As Sarah stared at his cabin, she was forced to admit that her feelings for Lucas went deeper than any infatuation.

Knocking firmly on his front door, she realized that she had no idea what she was going to say to him. But she couldn't let another week go by without seeing him, without hearing his voice.

The door swung open, and she met Julie Quincy's blue eyes. There was a moment of silence before Julie spoke.

"What are you doing here?"

"I—I want to talk to Lucas."

The girl scowled. "Why? Haven't you caused enough trouble?"

Sarah struggled for patience. Having to get past a hostile teenage gatekeeper was one obstacle she hadn't counted on. "Just tell Lucas I'm here, Julie. I'll wait for him outside."

"You broke his heart, you know."

Sarah couldn't help smiling. Perhaps she and Lucas were even, after all. "My heart isn't in such terrific shape, either."

"Julie, who are you talking to?" Lucas's voice reached them as they stood facing each other.

"Nobody."

The door slammed shut in Sarah's face, and two seconds later the porch light went out.

Now what? Did she have enough gumption to knock on Lucas's door twice?

The light came back on, and the door swung open again. Only this time, the gatekeeper was a frowning Lucas.

"Good."

"Wh-what?" Given his fierce expression, his comment was somewhat difficult to understand.

He closed the door and stepped outside. "I said 'good.'"

"Oh."

"I thought I heard your voice, and I'm relieved to know I wasn't hearing things."

That made sense. What didn't add up was the feeling of foreboding that washed over her. "I stopped by to...talk."

Lucas's face and eyes were as cold as they'd been a week earlier. "Yeah, I guess it's time." He glanced at his watch. "We better make it quick. In a few minutes, I'll be on my way to Spokane."

"Tonight?"

"Something came up."

Are you coming back? "I see."

"We might as well cut to the bottom line."

"Yes, I suppose we should."

"I'm sorry, Sarah. I know I hurt you. I didn't mean to, you know." For a moment his eyes softened. Then he cleared his throat. "I guess I never told you that I saw you a couple of times before we met that morning in the cove. The thing is I've had the hots for you for a long time."

The "hots" for her?

"Anyway, after we met, one thing led to another. I wanted you. A summer affair sounded damned appealing. When you said you liked shy, sensitive types, I thought I might as well take advantage of your preference." He laughed harshly. "Hell, I'm a builder. I was just customizing myself to fit your specifications. In my trade, it's something I do all the time. Understand?"

Sarah nodded. She couldn't speak. A hard lump had formed in her throat.

"Being the smart lady that you are, you caught on to my game before I could..." His voice had thickened. For the second time, he cleared his throat. "Do I have to spell it out for you?"

"No..."

He glanced at his watch again. "Look, I've got to get out of here."

"I—I didn't mean to—to keep you."

"Sarah..."

She looked up.

"Was there...was there something you wanted to tell me?"

"Just that I—I'm sorry I signed the contract with Brewster. I know you wanted to—to help me build the camp."

Lucas took a step toward Sarah, then stopped himself. He'd committed himself to this course. He wouldn't back down.

"No problem. I checked Brewster out. He's a redneck, but he'll do a good job. The truth is, my company doesn't usually handle such small projects. You did us both a favor picking another builder." *And I'm going to do us both a favor by getting out of your life.*

"Th-then I guess there's nothing more to say."

"Sarah, I—" He couldn't help himself. He reached out and pulled her into his arms, bringing his mouth hungrily against hers.

For a few timeless moments, he let her warm him. But when her arms came up around his neck and her body pressed against his, he knew he was going to have to say goodbye to such warmth.

"Oh, baby..." He gripped her wrists and pulled her arms down. "There's no time for us now. I'll be back before fall. We'll have time then for...a roll in the sack."

He felt her stiffen against him and had to clench his jaw to keep from calling back his words. He had to get out of here. There was a dying old man who needed him.

She said nothing. She simply turned from him and walked into the night. The cold cut through Lucas, and he'd never felt more alone.

He knew one fact for sure—doing the right thing felt like hell. And who would have guessed that hell was so damned cold?

Chapter Eleven

Sarah dipped her paintbrush into a bucket of strawberry-colored paint. More than six weeks had passed since Lucas had walked out of her life.

Using smooth strokes, she continued to paint the bungalow's thoroughly scraped exterior. Lucas's coarse reference to lovemaking still haunted her. That she had meant so little to him cut deeply.

Three more strokes of the brush brought her to the corner of the frame building. Looking up, she discovered she'd painted as high as she could reach without a ladder. She laid aside the paintbrush.

From the shady corner where she'd been working, she stepped into the sunshine. Carpenters, trucks and materials filled the landscape. Odell Brewster certainly knew how to get the job done. He'd approached the building and remodeling project as if he were a general and inactivity the enemy. The troops had definitely been marshaled.

The sound of hammers, saws, stapling guns and drills made the silence that used to surround the lake only a memory. Sarah quickly stepped aside to avoid a forklift loaded with panels of sheet rock. She had to pick her way carefully through curling mounds of black extension cords to get to the motor home. When she reached it, the door swung open and Deborah emerged.

Sarah looked at her partner's crisp white shorts, immaculate peach-colored T-shirt and sighed. "Do you *have* to look so perfect?"

She watched as Deborah's eyes took in the paint-spattered, yellow bandanna that covered her dark hair. She could feel the drying flecks of pink paint that decorated her face, and she could see the wet, pink spots on her clothes.

"No need to ask what you've been doing. You do realize we're paying good money to have the workmen do our painting?"

Sarah glanced down at her cutoffs and red halter top. "There's no way I can sit back and just watch. I have to be a part of all of it." With paint-smeared fingers, she gestured to the semiorganized pandemonium that engulfed the clearing.

"I know, honey. That's what makes you . . . you."

"Thanks . . . I think. Where are you headed?"

"I'm on my way to Lucas's cabin. Wendy and Julie can't seem to get enough of each other's company. They probably stayed up until midnight giggling and talking about boys. Now they want to go into town and see that new Keaton film."

At the mention of Lucas's name, Sarah tuned out Deborah's explanation. Though she hadn't seen him in over a month, she had been aware of the huge truck with Rockworth Construction emblazoned across it in ten-foot letters that had pulled onto his property. The immediate area around his cabin had also become a zone of activity.

"We'd invite you to join us, Sarah. But the movie starts in forty minutes, and I don't think you could make yourself presentable in anything under two hours.'

"Uh...all right. I'll see you later."

"What are you going to do?"

"Get a drink and then find a ladder," she answered absently.

"Sarah, you can't go on like this."

"Why not? We're doing great. Camp Grey Horse will be officially open in two weeks."

"Julie says Lucas might be coming back today."

Sarah tensed, her fatigue and thirst instantly forgotten. "It's a free country. As long as he stays on his property, we won't have any problems."

"Has it occurred to you that in your own way you're every bit as stubborn as your brother?"

"Of course not. Ryan's a pigheaded mule, and I'm eminently reasonable."

"Oh, honey," Deborah lamented. "If you weren't covered in pink paint, I'd give you a hug."

"Better save the hug. I'd make a mess of you."

Later, when she was lugging the unwieldy wood ladder back to the bungalow, Sarah thought about Deborah's suggestion that she was cut from the same tough fabric as Ryan. The idea was absurd. She was a mild little mouse compared to her fire-breathing dragon of a brother.

Sarah came to a stop and stared blankly at the wall of the bungalow that should have been half painted. It wasn't. A shirtless workman with a tan as dark as pine bark stood beside the freshly painted wall. He was adjusting the nozzle of an industrial-size paint sprayer.

He looked up from his task. "Can I help you, ma'am?"

"Uh, no. . . ." Sarah put down the ladder and eyed the flawless pink wall. "You work fast."

"You bet. Come back in twenty minutes and I'll have the whole building painted, and it won't take much longer to do the white trim."

She didn't doubt him. "That'll be great."

Sarah turned away, looking at the building site with fresh eyes. It was demoralizing to realize she'd been in the way. She should have gone to the movie with Deborah.

Dejectedly she tucked a loose strand of hair under her bandanna, moving instinctively toward the quiet of the beckoning forest. Naturally her thoughts were dominated by the man she didn't want to think about.

She missed Lucas. Life wasn't nearly as fun and . . . significant without him. Sarah nudged a pine cone from the faint path she'd picked to follow. *Significant* seemed a strange word to use in describing Lucas's impact on her life. She began to poke and pull at the word, scarcely noticing when the tiny trail she followed ceased to exist and she walked on a random course through the thickening trees.

Important. . . . Lucas had become very important to the quality of her life. She supposed that was an understandable way to feel about a man one had fallen in love with.

Essential. . . .

Sarah smiled. That was the word. Lucas Rockworth had become essential to her.

And he was a rat. The smile wobbled, then faded. She was in love with a rat. At that admission, Sarah

paused. The frenzied sounds of construction had become barely distinguishable through the dense shelter
of the forest. It just wasn't fair that she should still be
in love with him.

She began to walk again, wanting to run, to shout,
to pull at her hair and rail at fate. She didn't want to
love a hard, tough man like Lucas. She wanted someone gentle and tender and…and decent. Someone who
believed in commitment.

After a large amount of time and distance had been
dispensed with, Sarah gradually became aware of the
immense quiet that blanketed the woods. She turned
slowly and faced the way she'd come. Silent pines met
her gaze. There was no path, just a carpet of faintly
flattened pine needles lying across dark earth.

She refused to be lost. She had an excellent sense of
direction.

The trees weren't so thick that she couldn't see the
sun. Its rays had been on her face as she had walked,
so now she would return with its heat against her back.
She'd head downhill. Even if she missed her property, she would find the lake. Once there, it would be
an easy matter to get home.

A squirrel's raucous chattering broke the silence.
The animal seemed vastly irritated about something
and was telling the whole world about it.

She glanced in the direction the racket was coming
from and caught her breath. Through a stand of trees
on her left, she glimpsed a lush green glen. Sunlight
seemed to spill from the sky above it. Sarah felt
something pull her toward the serene clearing.

Not stopping to analyze what compelled her, she
moved toward the hidden glen. Standing between
herself and the clearing was an almost impenetrable
barrier of dense pine. She actually had to turn side-

ways to squeeze through the last couple of trees blocking her path. When she stepped into the small meadow, she inhaled a sharp breath.

So much beauty surrounded Lake Grey Horse, she'd become accustomed to it—to the blue skies, a sparkling lake, timbered forests and crests of distant mountains. But as she stared around the secluded clearing, she found herself enchanted by its perfection. Wildflowers, grass, trees, sky, and a meandering mountain creek—all combined to form a visual feast.

A feeling of peace swept through her. She felt cocooned by her surroundings. As if perhaps she'd stepped into another dimension.

She moved deeper into the magical glen. The rest of the world could have ceased to exist, so isolated and protected did she feel. She turned in a circle, cherishing the strange, sweet calm that seemed to drench the still air.

Tipping her face skyward, she closed her eyes. And somehow she felt as if she could see the next thirty years of her life—facing the challenges provided by marriage to a strong-willed man, a man who would cherish and protect her with his own life.

Lucas...

Instantly Sarah's eyes snapped open. Where had that thought sprang from? She certainly wasn't going to marry *him*. And he had made it abundantly clear that marriage had been the last thing on his mind.

The sound of the rushing stream made Sarah conscious of a deep thirst. She moved toward the water and knelt beside it, dipping her cupped hand into its clear channel. Water dribbled between her fingers and down her chin. Wiping her mouth with the back of her hand, she sat back on her knees.

When would the hole in her heart begin to mend?

During the past few weeks, she'd cried her tears and reconciled herself to Lucas being as stubborn and iron willed as Ryan. But she couldn't reconcile herself to him misleading her just so he could get her into bed.

Moodily she stared into the distance, oblivious to her surroundings. She was looking into the past and remembering when they'd met. Mamma bear had chased her from her camp, and she'd jumped into space.

Lucas had caught her. What were the odds of something like that happening?

And then there's been that ferocious bee. Lucas's quick thinking had provided immediate relief from the pain.

She remembered their midnight swim and shivered. His second kiss... The brief passion that had burned between them made a mockery of her visions of him as a timid lover.

And the poetry... Even with a broken heart, she discovered it was possible to smile.

Recalling the way he'd pitched in with the designs for Camp Grey Horse, the smile faded. He'd helped her stake out the new buildings, and it had been his architect's plans that Brewster had used to build the camp.

And when Wendy had arrived at the lake, bound by her wheelchair, Lucas had promptly built ramps to his cabin. Whatever his motives, Lucas Rockworth had been generous.

Whatever his motives...

He'd said he'd wanted to get her into bed. And yet... And yet, she recalled several occasions when she'd been his for the taking, and he hadn't...taken....

So who was the real Lucas Rockworth?

Sarah's brooding gaze moved across the stream and settled on dense bowers of mountain underbrush. Gradually she realized she was looking at a small log cabin virtually overrun by the growth that had camouflaged it from her view.

The old house looked like a pioneer homestead. Authentic. Probably a hundred years old. Sarah rose slowly, absently brushing the grit from her knees.

So old, so... abandoned? No, the log home looked as if it were merely waiting. Waiting for its family to return. From where she stood, the antique structure looked as if it had been undisturbed for a century. It looked strong. As if it's been build to last several generations.

Scanning the creek bank cutting between her and the cabin, Sarah estimated it a foot too wide for her to jump. Maybe if she took a running leap? She backed up.

A hand clamped down on her bare shoulder, and she screamed.

"Even someone as impetuous as you, Sarah Burke, wouldn't try to jump this stream."

"Lucas!" She found herself spun around to face a grim-featured dragon.

"In the flesh," he observed tersely. "You're trespassing."

She raised her chin, pride coming to her rescue. "Are you making a citizen's arrest?"

"Wandering from a well-traveled path is a guaranteed way to get lost. And getting lost in this rugged terrain is a surefire way to get yourself killed, Sarah."

"I'm not lost. I can find my way back to the lake."

"Have a good sense of direction, do you?"

"Excellent," she affirmed stoutly.

"I think I'm beginning to understand why your brother is so overprotective. You're an angel who definitely needs her wings clipped."

"Are you volunteering for the job?" She held her breath. From Lucas's past behavior, she should have been nervous. But strangely enough, his motives no longer worried her.

"It would be for your own good."

"I've discovered that when someone says something's for my own good, it generally... hurts."

Touching her loosely knotted bandanna, he gently tugged the ends apart and slid it from her head. He tucked the yellow square into his pocket.

Sarah shivered, feeling oddly exposed with a gentle breeze teasing her freed hair.

"I think we both have the power to hurt each other." He extended a strong hand. "Come sit with me on the grass."

Feeling that it was impossible to do otherwise, she slipped her hand into his. He dropped to his knees and pulled her next to him. Taking a moment to find a comfortable position, he rested his back against the smooth bark of a felled tree. Then he fitted her to him so her head rested against his shoulder. They faced the stream and cabin beyond it.

"The first time I saw you was in your brother's office. You were wearing a dark and dreary business suit, and your hair was scrunched into a dark bump on the back of your head."

"It's called a chignon," Sarah corrected gently. "I don't remember seeing you in Ryan's office."

"You never looked in my direction. You were too busy hand delivering the penalty check to your brother. It was obvious you were upset—as if the money were coming from your own pocket. I remember thinking what a proud woman you must be, to be so disturbed at settling that debt.''

''The money *was* from my pocket, or at any rate my bank account. Ryan insisted that I personally bear the financial burden of the penalty, because I'd been the one to talk Deborah out of selling her land.''

''That check came from you, not Burke Realty?'' he asked in surprise.

She nodded.

''Teaching you a lesson, was he?''

''For my own good, you understand?''

''Ouch. Forget what I said about clipping your wings for your own good. We'll clip them for my benefit.''

''*That's* supposed to make me feel better?''

Lucas took her hand and pressed it to his mouth. ''Doesn't it?''

She tried to ignore the hot and icy tingles careening from her fingertips to the tips of her breasts. Too clearly etched in her memory was the last time she'd spoken with Lucas, when he'd told her he had only pursued her with an affair in mind.

''Sarah, don't pull away from me.'' His hand tightened on hers. ''I know I deserve it for the way I acted when you came to my cabin, but don't give up on me yet.''

Even if she'd wanted to, she didn't know if she could give up on him. ''What is it you want to tell me?''

''That I'm not noble. I'm not kind. I'm not . . . I'm not Mr. Rogers.''

Sarah commanded herself not to smile. ''No kidding.''

''But I'm not a bad person, either.''

Studying his serious features, she nodded. "I know."

"The reason I left the lake that night was that my father had had a heart attack." Lucas's eyes took on a distant expression. "I've been with him for the past six weeks. He's going to make it. And . . . and I've resolved a lot of the anger I've felt toward him."

She laced her fingers with his. "I'm glad for you."

"That night when I opened the door and saw you standing on the porch, all of a sudden it hit me. You deserved a helluva lot better man than I could ever be—a man like the one you thought I was."

"So you decided to—to—"

"To play the part of a real cad, someone you could walk away from without looking back."

Sarah thought back to that night. His plan should have worked, and yet she'd been unable to forget him, even after the cutting things he'd said.

"Anyway, after spending this time with my father, I discovered I don't want to end up alone. That whatever it takes, you're going to fall in love with the real Lucas Rockworth."

"Am I?"

"Yeah. The point is, Sarah, you're too strong a woman to become involved with a weak man."

"I see."

"You're a feminine version of Ryan, only you don't seem to realize it."

"Someone else recently made that observation."

"They were right. And a tough, strong woman needs a man who'll keep her on her toes. Understand?"

"Absolutely."

His eyes darkened, and it was as if he clearly saw her for the first time. "Ah, Sarah—all covered in pink paint. I want to find where every drop of it has fallen."

Gently he tumbled her onto the mountain grass. Then he covered her body with his. "The first time I saw you, you intrigued me. The second time I think I became your slave."

His husky growl shimmered across her nerve endings. "The—the second time?"

"At the ball Quincy Enterprises hosted. You wore silver. Slinky...sexy...silver." He punctuated his words with hot commando kisses that stung her throat.

"You were there? I don't remember—"

A tender love bite on her shoulder silenced the words. "Then I'll remember...for both of us. You were ravishing, a sensuous siren. And I wanted you. Even before."

"Be-before?"

"Why, Sarah, are you repeating me again?"

"I think so." She let her eyelids drift shut, to more fully experience the wonder of it all.

"Good." His deep voice throbbed with male satisfaction. "I wanted you before I knew you were both angel *and* adventurer. Before I knew dreamers and stargazers still abounded. Before..."

She opened her eyes and found herself both enchanted and caught. Enchanted by the discovery that her warrior could speak the words of a poet. And caught by a smoldering hunger that left her breathless. "Yes?"

"Before I knew I loved you."

His mouth possessed hers. With thorough, absolute mastery. Sarah felt the cool grass press against her bare back and the heat of Lucas's frame against each curve she possessed. It seemed that every part of her there was to touch, Lucas touched. And stroked. And caressed.

Somehow her halter top became unfastened. Lucas's mouth feasted upon her exposed flesh. Sarah quivered and trembled and ached. She'd thought she'd known passion before in Lucas's embrace, but that passion was of yesterday. Today... It was what she experienced in his arms today that mattered.

"Oh, Lord, you're beautiful. I want you so much, honey. I love you so much."

"Lucas, oh, Lucas..." His words, his touch became her world. There was no yesterday. There was only now, this moment, this man—this today.

"What, honey?" he murmured as his lips and tongue sampled, tasted.

"Do you, do you have...?"

His teeth delicately raked a coral bud. "I have everything you need, honey."

"...your epi-pen?"

It took a moment for him to make sense of her question. "Why?"

"Because I hear a buzzing that doesn't have anything to do with how well you kiss."

Lucas sat up.

Sarah's hands automatically moved to cover her breasts.

"Oh, Lord, honey. Don't do that. Let me see you."

"But—"

"Forget the bee. I've got my antitoxin. Ten thousand bees couldn't keep me from sharing this moment with you." He made quick work of unbuttoning his shirt. Then he gently pulled her to him. "You feel so good. Both soft and hard, diamond hard."

The intimacy went beyond words. Sarah buried her face against Lucas's naked shoulder.

"I'd sell Rockworth Construction lock, stock, and barrel for a flashlight."

Lucas's work-roughened palms stroked the sensitive flesh of her back, sending shock waves skittering through her. "A flashlight?"

He chuckled. "Not what most experts suggest a prepared man should carry. But in our situation, we're finished without one."

Sarah stared at him in bemusement.

"It's getting late, and there's no way we can find our way back to the lake in the dark."

"Oh."

He stood and pulled her to her feet. Sarah tried not to be self-conscious as he helped her into her halter top. After he put his shirt on, they moved toward the spot where they'd entered the magical glade. When they'd stepped through the trees that seemed to guard it, she put her hand in his arm.

"We'll never be able to find this place again, will we?"

Briefly he studied the surrounding area and the perimeter of dense pines that closed off the meadow. "Probably not, honey."

"There's something special about it, Lucas. Did you feel it?"

"When I walked into that clearing, I was madder than blazes that you would wander out here alone. But five minutes alone with you in there, and all I could think about was how much I . . . I loved you."

Sarah met his proud, honest gaze. "Five minutes alone with you in there and . . ."

"And?"

"And I knew that even though you weren't the man I thought I should fall in love with, I . . . loved you."

"It took you long enough to say it."

"I was working up my courage."

"We've learned a lot from each other. You taught me that I had a softer, more gentle side than I realized. And I showed you that you have the makings of—"

"Of what? A tyrant?"

Grinning, he pulled her into his arms. "I guess there's always that risk. You do have a tendency to bully."

He stopped her protest with a kiss. Then another. And another. When he had her lips throbbing, he drew back.

"Marry me, Sarah Burke. Take me to paradise and share it with me for as long as we both shall live."

"That hardly seems long enough," Sarah whispered.

"No it doesn't." He kissed her long and hard. "But it's more than I ever dreamed possible."

Sarah cupped his face between her hands. "Can't we mark a path to the meadow? I'd like to come back someday."

He kissed her once more, then reached into his back pocket and pulled out her yellow bandanna, tying it to the low branch of a nearby pine. "This will have to do."

He put his arm around her, and they began walking toward the lake. And toward all the tomorrows with which a kindly fate would bless them.

* * * * *

Silhouette Romance®

COMING NEXT MONTH

#712 HARVEY'S MISSING—Peggy Webb
A Diamond Jubilee Title!
Janet Hall was in search of her missing weekend dog, Harvey, but what she found was Dan Albany, who claimed Harvey was *his* week*day* dog. Would the two ever agree on anything?

#713 JUST YOU AND ME—Rena McKay
The Loch Ness monster was less elusive than the blue-eyed MacNorris men of Norbrae Castle. Vacationing Lynn Marquet was falling fast for Mike MacNorris, one of the mystifying Scottish clansmen . . . or was she?

#714 MONTANA HEAT—Dorsey Kelley
Nanny Tracy Wilborough expected to find peace of mind in Montana. What she hadn't counted on was exciting rodeo performer Nick Roberts lassoing her heart!

#715 A WOMAN'S TOUCH—Brenda Trent
When Troy Mayhan first met neighbor Shelly Hall, they literally fell into each other's arms. Now the sexy ex-football player was determined to have her fall again—in love with him!

#716 JUST NEIGHBORS—Marcine Smith
Loner Wyatt Neville had never had a sweet tooth—or been tempted to indulge in romance—until delectable Angela Cowan moved her cookie factory next door to his home. . . .

#717 HIS BRIDE TO BE—Lisa Jackson
The contract said she was his bride to be for two weeks only. But two weeks was all it took for Hale Donovan to know that Valerie Pryce was his love for a lifetime.

AVAILABLE THIS MONTH:

AVAILABLE NOW—

the books you've been waiting for by one of
America's top romance authors!

DIANA PALMER

DUETS

Ten years ago Diana Palmer published her very first
romances. Powerful and dramatic, these gripping tales
of love are everything you have come to expect from
Diana Palmer.

This month some of these titles are available again in
DIANA PALMER DUETS—a special three-book collection. Each book has two wonderful stories plus an introduction by the author. You won't want to miss them!

Book 1
SWEET ENEMY
LOVE ON TRIAL

Book 2
STORM OVER THE LAKE
TO LOVE AND CHERISH

Book 3
IF WINTER COMES
NOW AND FOREVER

Available now at your favorite retail outlet.

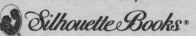 *Silhouette Books*®

DP-1A